The Yellow Rose Bush

By

Karen Lockley

For my mother,

Patricia

Based on a true story

CHAPTER ONE

I lifted my suitcase into the boot of the car, which I then slammed shut. Once I was in the driver's seat, I tapped the address of the hotel into my satnav and slipped my new Kings of Leon CD which Ben had bought me for Christmas, into the CD player. I then turned the key in the ignition, turned up the volume and eased the gear stick into reverse.

It was a dark but clear December evening. There's nothing quite like the feeling of taking to the open road, putting miles and miles between you and everyone else, and everything else you know.

"I'm sorry, but I won't be here to see the New Year in with you now I'm afraid," I had told Jayne only yesterday. Jayne was my best and oldest friend. Our children had grown up together. They were almost like brother and sister, or at the very least, close cousins. In fact Jayne's daughter, Sarah still called me Auntie Fay and Ben always referred to Jayne with the same fondness and familiarity.

"Why, where are you going?" asked Jayne.

"I'm going away to North Wales for a little while," I said. "I'll be staying in a quaint little hotel. It's really not that far away at all."

"How long have you known this?" Jayne asked, with a tinge of irritation in her voice.

"I only booked it last night. I did it online."

"Who are you going with?"

"No one."

Jayne's eyes widened. "Why?"

"Because I just need to get away. Somewhere on my own. To get my head together, you know? And hopefully work on my book without any other distractions."

Jayne let out a deep sigh. "Well I can't say that I'm not disappointed, but if that's what you need to do.........."

I knew Jayne would understand. One thing I could always count on was Jayne's support, whether she agreed with me or not. Ben's reaction on the other hand indicated he probably didn't know me as well as he thought, or understand me as well as Jayne did.

"You know you would have been welcome to stay with us if you needed to get away," he'd said.

"I know," I'd replied. "And I know you and Anita would have made me more than welcome. But this is something I need to do."

"I'm just a bit worried about you being on your own, Mom."

"Don't be," I assured him. "I'll be fine, honestly. Besides, if I hate it, there's nothing

to stop me from coming back early."

"Will you ring me or text me to let me know you've arrived there safely?" asked Ben.

"Of course I will."

∞

By the time I reached the hotel I was dog tired. It hadn't been a particularly long journey but I'd had a busy day and had slept very little the night before. Not that that was unusual. I couldn't remember the last time I had enjoyed a decent night's sleep.

Initially I drove straight past the hotel because it didn't look like a hotel at all from the outside. Instead it had the appearance of a small gothic church. As I struggled to get through the doorway with its large heavy wooden door, the young man at the reception desk hurried over to assist me. He looked about the same age as Ben, tall like him but with much darker features. He was wearing a smart black shirt buttoned up to the neck with matching black trousers.

"I have a reservation," I explained. The young man went back behind his desk.

"Is your name Reynolds?" he asked as he checked his computer.

"Yes, Fay Reynolds."

"You're in room 12," he said. "I'll just give you a hand with your bags."

I followed the young man along a narrow corridor and up a short flight of stairs. He opened the door of room 12 and dragged my suitcase inside. "Okay?"

"Yes, lovely, thank you," I said, taking a panoramic mental shot of the room.

"Breakfast is between seven and nine-thirty," he smiled, as he handed me a key and left.

After I finished unpacking, I made myself a cup of tea and got undressed for bed. I sat up in bed for a little while to read. I was close to finishing James Patterson's *Honeymoon.* It was after I realised that I couldn't remember the last two paragraphs that I had read when I decided to put the book down and try to get some sleep. I snuggled down under the covers, the cool crisp sheets comforting against my skin. The bed probably wasn't as comfortable as my one at home, the mattress rather too firm and unyielding, but nevertheless I felt more relaxed than I had felt in a long time. Away from home. Away from him.

I had just closed my eyes when my mobile phone vibrated and whistled to alert me to an incoming message. "Shit!" I exclaimed, sitting bolt upright in bed as I remembered my promise to let Ben know I had arrived safely. I turned on the bedside lamp and picked up the phone. Sure enough it was a text from Ben.....

I haven't heard from you. Please let me know you're ok xxx

I immediately replied.....

Hi Ben, I arrived safely and I'm fine. So sorry I didn't let you know straight away. It seems to be a nice hotel and I think I'll get some writing done here. Speak soon. Love to you all xxx

I felt a bit like an inconsiderate teenager who had forgotten to check in with her parents. Then I received another text from Ben which not only made me smile, but made me wonder if Ben really did know me after all.*As long as you're okay. Hope this break turns out to be just what you need. Love you Mom xxx*

CHAPTER TWO

Despite my initial hopes and expectations, I slept fitfully that night. But I was determined to get up for breakfast. When I drew back the curtains the following morning, it was barely daylight and the rain drenched streets seemed to shimmer like rivers in the glow of the street lights. Everything looked grey. "What a rotten morning," I muttered to myself.

I made my way down to the restaurant for breakfast at around a quarter to nine. "Table just for one?" asked the waitress breezily as I entered the dining area.

"Yes, just one."

"Is this okay?" she asked, pointing towards a table which was already laid for one. Probably the only table laid just for one.

"Yes, that's fine," I said.

As I sat down at the table, the waitress handed me the breakfast menu. "Would you like tea or coffee?"

"Coffee, please."

"There's also fruit juices, cereals and pastries on the table over there," she said, nodding towards a long table which stood against the length of one of the walls. "Help yourself if you wish."

"Thank you." I smiled at the waitress who smiled back before leaving to fetch my coffee.

I glanced around the dining room. It was fairly small but tastefully decorated with subdued lighting and comfortable high back leather chairs at the tables. There were just four other people seated for breakfast. A young attractive couple, possibly married, possibly not. Either way, they seemed happy and relaxed in one another's company. Then there was an older couple. Much older. They were sat opposite one another but rarely seemed to look up from their breakfasts to engage in any conversation, however brief. I was sure this couple were married and had probably been married for a very long time. Three young women then entered the room, chatting and giggling as they made their way over to one of the other vacant tables.

As I sat alone at my table, I was quite surprised to find that none of these people seemed to give me so much as a cursory glance. I knew that if it were me, I would wonder why a woman was breakfasting alone in a hotel during the holiday period. In an attempt to conceal my discomfort, I tried to focus on my own thoughts, telling myself, *I can enjoy my own company, without feeling a need to engage in meaningless small talk. I can just be me. And right now, me is all I need.*

A couple of minutes later, the waitress returned with my coffee. "Would you like to order any hot food?" she asked.

"Yes, could I have the scrambled eggs with toast please?"

"Would you like white or brown bread?"

"White, please," I replied, as I handed her the menu.

I picked up the cup of fresh filtered coffee and held it between my hands with my elbows resting on the table. I drank in its rich aroma before I even brought the cup to my lips. Then as I stared through the window before me at the relentless falling rain, my thoughts wandered back through the years, farther and farther back until I was at the party where it all began.....

CHAPTER THREE

We met at a party all those years ago. I had seen Adam around the town a couple of times before but never knew his name, and had never dared to hope that he would be interested in someone like me. I hadn't even realised that he had been invited to the party until Jayne and I arrived there around nine o'clock in the evening. "Oh my God, he's here!" I exclaimed in a loud whisper.

"Who?"

"Him....that gorgeous bloke I was telling you about with the dark wavy hair."

"Where?"

"He's standing by the woman in the red dress," I said, managing to avoid pointing in his direction. "Don't make it obvious you are looking though."

"Well how can I see him if I don't look?" laughed Jayne.

"You can look, but just don't make it too obvious."

Nonchalantly, Jayne began to scan the room with her eyes until she fixed her gaze on him.

"Yes, very nice," Jayne approved. "Why don't you go over and talk to him?"

"No, I can't. He wouldn't be interested in me. Besides, he may already have a girlfriend."

"I suggested talking to him, not throwing yourself at him."

"Maybe a bit later. When I've had a couple more drinks."

About an hour or so later, I was pouring myself another glass of white wine in the kitchen when suddenly he was beside me. I could still hear *The Jam* playing on the turntable in the sitting room. I felt a ripple within of both excitement and trepidation. He was standing so close I could smell him, clean and fresh like crisp laundered cotton, mixed with the delicate scent of sandalwood. He reached out for a glass and touched my hand briefly with his, sending another ripple through my body. "I didn't know you were a friend of Dave's," he said. His voice was soft yet masculine.

"I don't really know Dave," I explained, still not looking at him. The party was in Dave's flat but it wasn't him who had invited me. "I'm a friend of Peter's though."

"Oh, I see," he said. "Would you like *us* to be friends?"

Rather a cheesy line I thought but I could not help but turn my head to look at him now. He was slightly taller than me. His eyes were so big and blue, fringed with long black lashes, too long for a man really. He was smiling and his eyes seemed to twinkle as he gazed into mine. I couldn't help but smile back, but then lowered my head coyly. I felt the blood surge through my veins and my face flush crimson.

"Why are you blushing?" he teased. This of course made me blush all the more.

"I'm not," I said, bashfully, knowing full well I was. My head still lowered, I lifted my eyes only, noticing several dark wisps of hair emerging from the opening in his shirt, which was unbuttoned at the neck and I observed, had the second button missing. He then leaned forward towards me, so that I felt his breath on my skin. I vaguely remember thinking that his behaviour was rather inappropriate. He had barely spoken to me and already he was trying to kiss me. Nevertheless, I didn't mind, and not just because I'd already had several glasses of wine, but because I was in awe of his beauty. I had never met a man so handsome before who actually wanted to kiss me. So as he leaned towards me, I lifted my head and closed my eyes. I felt his soft but firm lips press against mine, parting them as he did so. His hand then encircled my waist, pulling me closer to him. I lifted my right hand and ran my fingers through his thick black wavy locks. His hair was surprisingly soft. I felt his tongue gently explore the inside of my mouth. I then did the same, tentatively at first, caressing his tongue with mine. An electric current shot through my body and I suddenly felt weak and light headed. I was sure that if he were to let me go at that moment, I would simply crumple to the floor. When I describe it now, it all sounds rather scary and unpleasant, but it wasn't. In fact, it was nothing less than wonderful. I had never been kissed like this before. I had never felt like this before, and I don't think I ever did again. Nothing really compared to that first pure, delicious kiss.

I was disappointed when he stopped; but he wanted to say something. "My name's Adam, by the way." His arm was still around my waist as his eyes gazed, almost unblinking into mine.

"I'm Fay," I said, my voice barely above a whisper.

CHAPTER FOUR

I didn't go home that night. Instead I went back to Adam's place. I had only just met him and really knew nothing about him; he could have been a mad axe murderer for all I knew; but when you're young, a little drunk and in love you don't tend to worry too much about such things. And yes, I think I *was* in love. From the very moment he kissed me.

I was slightly impressed that he had his own house, whereas I still lived at home with my dad. That night however I had planned to stay over at Jayne's as she lived just around the corner from Dave's house. Adam's house was really rather lovely and had a cottagey feel about it. The rooms were fairly small but cosy. Adam selected an LP from his rather impressive collection on the floor that lined one of the sitting room walls and placed it on the turntable. I then followed Adam into the kitchen where he proceeded to fill the kettle from the sink tap. I took two mugs from the mug tree as I glanced around the kitchen. The fitted cupboards were made of antique pine. "This is nice," I remarked. "Do you live here alone?"

"Yes I do," said Adam. Suddenly he turned around and put his arms around me, smiling. "Let's go upstairs."

"What about the coffee?" I asked, innocently.

"Never mind that. We can have the coffee later."

In silence, I followed Adam upstairs. I may have appeared calm, but inside I was a whirlwind of emotions. I felt excited, but just a little bit scared as well I think. I wasn't in the habit of sleeping with someone on the first night. Adam let me into one of the bedrooms, which I assumed was his. He turned on the light as we entered to reveal a double bed, no doubt hastily made that morning, judging by the rather crumpled red duvet that covered it. Next to the bed stood a pine bedside table on which was placed a small lamp with a red shade. Adam went over to it and switched it on. He then turned off the main light. The bedside lamp emitted a warm subtle glow. Adam then took a couple of steps towards me and attempted to gently undress me. "How do you get this thing off?" he laughed softly.

I was wearing my new blue jumpsuit. It had cap sleeves and a low neckline revealing my modest cleavage. The silky material clung to my slim waist, falling from my hips into flattering wide palazzo legs. Smiling coyly, I turned around. "The zip is at the back," I whispered. The almost haunting sound of *Orchestral Manoeuvres in the Dark* floated up the stairs from the sitting room and as I felt Adam slowly unzip me, uttering not a single word, a shiver ran down my spine. I sensed Adam briefly and tantalisingly touch my hair which fell in soft golden waves below my shoulders, still boasting remnants of a perm and the henna I had dyed it with. I stepped out of the jumpsuit, then slid under the duvet before watching Adam take off his clothes. He seemed to have no inhibitions whatsoever. But then he had no reason to. He was perfect.

When I woke the next morning I was in bed alone, but I thought I could hear faint sounds from the kitchen; metal against china; a spoon being turned in a cup. I smiled to myself as I stretched. I had slept well. In fact it was probably the best sleep I had ever had. Then I heard Adam climbing the stairs. He entered the room with a steaming mug in each hand. He had made coffee. He was wearing a pair of grey jogging bottoms that hung loosely from his hips, but was naked on top. I stared admiringly at his body, his tanned slim torso.

In those days people didn't have mobile phones and it never occurred to me until that morning that Jayne might wonder where I was. I had forgotten to tell her where I was going. I was just swept up in the moment, you might say. "I will have to go soon," I said, as I sat up in bed, pulling the duvet up under my arms, so as to cover my naked breasts.

"Why?" asked Adam, carefully handing me one of the mugs. He didn't get back under the duvet but sat down beside me, his legs hanging over the edge of the bed.

"I was supposed to stay at Jayne's last night. Jayne's my friend," I explained. "She'll wonder where I am."

"Okay," said Adam, smiling. "You drink your coffee and then I'll drive you to Jayne's. Does she live far from here?"

"Oh no, not far. It's just round the corner from Dave's house. I could walk it from here."

"Then I'll walk with you," said Adam, smiling. "After you've had your coffee, you can use the shower if you like."

"Thanks," I said. "I will if you don't mind."

It was a lovely spring morning, and there was hardly a cloud in the sky. We walked hand in hand, without speaking, a chorus of invisible birds filling the silence with their melody.

"This is it," I said as we reached the gate to Jayne's house. We were still standing at the gate, kissing one another good-bye when Jayne appeared at the door, with one hand on her hip, wearing a rather stern expression.

"Can I call you later?"

I was quite surprised when Adam asked me this question. I think I must have assumed that in the cold light of day, Adam would realise that last night was never going to lead to anything more. I searched my handbag for a pen and paper. I didn't have a pen so I wrote my telephone number down on a till receipt with my eyeliner.

As soon as we got into Jayne's house she chided, "I've been worried sick about you. Where have you been?"

"With Adam," I smiled.

"Well you could have told me where you were going. You just disappeared. What was I supposed to think?"

"I'm sorry," I apologised sheepishly. "It all just happened too fast." If ever there was a time to use the expression *swept off my feet*, this was it.

"Have you had any breakfast?" Jayne asked.

"No, not yet."

"Would you like some toast?" I knew Jayne couldn't be mad at me for long.

"That'll be great," I said.

"And then you can tell me all about it," smiled Jayne.

CHAPTER FIVE

Later that day, sure enough, Adam telephoned me. "It's for you, Fay," said Dad. "I think he said his name was Adam."

"Thanks, Dad," I said, as he handed me the receiver. I turned away from Dad's quizzical gaze. "Hi, Adam." I found myself smiling bashfully, even though Adam clearly could not see me.

"Hi, Fay," said Adam. Just the sound of his voice made me tingle all over. "Do you fancy meeting up for a drink later? I can pick you up, say about seven?"

I was silent for a moment as I contemplated the prospect of going out drinking and stopping up late two evenings in a row. "Yeah, that'll be great," I finally replied. "I better give you my address."

"Okay, let me just get a pen and paper."

I then proceeded to reel off my address. "Do you know where that is?" I asked.

"Yes, I do," replied Adam. "Oh by the way, a friend of mine is getting tickets to see Bruce Springsteen. I wondered if you'd like to come?"

I'd never been to a concert before. "Yeah, I'd love to."

"Okay, I'll ask him to get two tickets for me then." I realised that after I hung up, I hadn't even asked Adam when the concert was. I suppose in those days I had a very flexible social calendar. I was very young and therefore did not really plan much in advance.

When Adam turned up at seven o'clock, I was still trying to decide what to wear. I had already changed about half a dozen times so as many outfits were still strewn over the bed or lay discarded on the floor. "Adam's here!" Dad called up the stairs.

"Won't be a moment!" I called back, trying not to betray in my voice the sheer panic I was now feeling.

Finally I settled for the first outfit I had tried on. As I made my way downstairs, I could hear Dad and Adam chatting in the sitting room. *They seem to be getting along well already*, I thought, smiling to myself.

When I entered the sitting room, Adam stood up to face me, smiling. Immediately I could feel myself blushing. He was wearing a black leather jacket and looked even more handsome than I remembered. "Are you ready?" he asked.

"Yes."

"Nice to meet you, Phillip," said Adam, courteously, holding out his hand to shake Dad's.

"You too," said Dad, smiling and shaking Adam's hand warmly. "What time do you think you'll be back, Fay?"

I looked at Adam. I didn't even know where we were going. "Probably about eleven," answered Adam. "Is that okay?"

"That's fine," said Dad. "Fay will tell you, I'm not that strict about things like that. I know Fay's a sensible girl. I just like to know, so I don't worry, you know?"

I think Dad gave me more credit than I deserved. I wasn't a wild child, or anything like that, but I was probably no more responsible than the average nineteen year old.

"Don't worry, she's in safe hands," said Adam.

"Where are we going?" I asked Adam as I slid into the passenger seat of his car. Not many people I knew around my age had a car of their own. Adam's was a blue Toyota corolla. For some reason, I would always remember that.

"I thought we'd go to the cinema first, if that's okay with you?" said Adam, as he turned the key in the ignition.

"Yeah, that'll be great. What's showing?"

"The Coal Miner's Daughter," replied Adam. "After that, I'd like you to meet some friends of mine. I've arranged to meet them in the White horse for a drink."

While we watched the film, Adam held my hand throughout. The last time I had been to the cinema was with someone called Barry. I couldn't even tell you what the film was about because we had spent the whole time snogging. But Adam was more mature than that. He was five years older than me, and it was refreshing to go to the cinema with someone who was actually interested in watching the film.

∞

"Did you enjoy the film?" asked Adam as we walked to the White horse which was just up the road from the cinema.

"Yeah," I replied. "It was a good film."

As we entered the pub, I remember thinking it was quite busy for a Sunday night. As we approached the far corner of the room, we were greeted by a group of Adam's friends. Sat at the large round table were half a dozen men and two women. They all looked around the same age as Adam. "This is Fay," said Adam, introducing me.

"Hi Fay!" they all replied, almost in unison.

They all shifted round the table to make a space for me. "Have a seat, Fay."

I sat down, feeling slightly awkward. "What would you like to drink?" Adam asked me.

"Er, um, can I have a rum and coke please?"

Adam went to the bar to get our drinks, leaving me alone with a bunch of perfect strangers. "My name's Mike," said the man who was sat rather uncomfortably close to me.

"Nice to meet you," I smiled. Mike had a pleasant face but was not as good looking as Adam. He was clean shaven with floppy light brown hair which was parted down the middle, and was wearing John Lennon style glasses. He was smartly dressed, wearing a brown suede blazer jacket over a white t-shirt and jeans. In time I learnt that what Mike lacked in vivacity and charm, he more than made up for in dependability and kindness.

I was relieved when Adam returned with our drinks, although by then I was already beginning to feel more relaxed. Adam's friends certainly made me feel welcome and Mike especially was very easy to talk to. "What do you do?" he had asked me.

"Oh, I just work in an office," I replied. "What about you?"

"I'm a Journalist."

"Really?" I said. "That sounds exciting."

"Not really," said Mike, smiling. "I only work for the local paper. I don't get to cover many big stories."

"You enjoy your job though, don't you?"

"Yeah, I got to admit I do, on the whole," said Mike. "How about you? Do you enjoy your job?"

"It's okay," I replied. "But typing invoices and ordering stationery is hardly my vocation."

"So what is your vocation?"

"Writing."

Mike raised an eyebrow. "What sort of stuff do you like to write?" he asked.

"Oh you know....stories.....poems. I'd love to write a novel one day."

"Really?" Mike seemed genuinely interested. Or was he merely surprised? I wasn't sure which.

"It's just a dream......."

"I tell you what," began Mike, "dreams are underrated. Without them, we'd probably still be living in caves. Don't ever give up on your dreams, Fay."

I smiled. Then Mike picked up a pack of cigarettes from the table and offered me one. "No, I'm okay, thanks," I said. Almost all of Adam's friends smoked, which in those days was not at all unusual.

Mike then introduced me to Julia who seemed eager to talk to me. She was sat next to Tony. Julia and Tony were already a couple. Julia seemed to go out of her way to make me feel at ease. She had long dark hair and was really quite beautiful, but I felt certain she didn't know it. "Have you known Adam a long time?" I asked her.

"Probably a couple of years," replied Julia, "but Tony's known him since they were at school together."

Julia and I chatted for a quite a while. She was a little older than Adam and Tony, and was a teacher, but she seemed more interested in learning about me than talking about herself. Before we knew it, it was last orders. It was only ten thirty but that was the norm for a Sunday night. Eventually I arrived home with Adam at around eleven, just as he had promised my dad.

As we stood on the path outside the house kissing one another good-bye, Adam said, "I can't see you tomorrow I'm afraid as I think I'll be working late, but if you're free Tuesday, we could go out again if you like?"

"That would be nice," I said, smiling.

Adam seemed pensive for a moment. "On second thoughts," began Adam, "why don't I pick you about seven, and you can come round to my place? I can cook us a nice meal."

"You can cook?"

"Well of course," said Adam, smiling. "I *do* need to eat sometimes."

I smiled back. I was beginning to get accustomed to what I can only describe as, his sarcastic style of humour.

After we kissed good-bye for the final time, I rather reluctantly entered the house, closing the door behind me. Already I was counting down the minutes and the hours before I would see Adam again.

CHAPTER SIX

It was Tuesday, and almost seven o'clock. This time I was ready when Adam arrived. In fact I was ready particularly early, partly because I had decided on the Monday what I was going to wear. The outfit I had chosen consisted of a pair of black leggings with bright yellow leg warmers and a matching loose fitting yellow t-shirt, adorned with strings of black and yellow plastic beads. To top it all, I had tied a thin yellow scarf in my hair. It conjures up a rather scary image of a giant canary, but was probably very fashionable in the 1980s. I certainly remember thinking that I was the bee's knees at the time.

Adam cooked Spaghetti Bolognese. It was the first time I had eaten Italian food so I had nothing to compare it with, but it was delicious. I remember having to concentrate very hard however so as not to spill it down my bright yellow t-shirt. We drank lots of wine which was probably a big mistake, considering I was at work the next day. Adam tried to persuade me to stay over which more than anything I wanted to do, but was still considerate enough not to yield to temptation. I didn't wish to cause Dad any unnecessary worry. I did return home a little late however when Adam dropped me off in a taxi.

It was almost too painful to say good-bye. I'd never felt such an unbelievably strong yearning before to be with someone all of the time. And as the weeks went by, I found that every day and every hour that I wasn't with him, I would be thinking of him, wanting him.

"Sorry I'm late," I said to Dad, trying really hard to look and sound as normal as possible, despite the fact that I could hear myself slurring my words and could barely focus on the blurred image of Dad who was stood before me in the kitchen.

"That's okay, darling. You're not very late." I smiled and turned to head upstairs to bed, hoping to escape before he realised I was so pissed. "Did you have a nice time?"

"Yes, thanks," I replied, turning back to face him and then leaning against the pantry door so as not to topple over.

"Wasn't Adam cooking you dinner?" Dad filled the kettle at the sink and then switched it on.

"Yeah, he did." Dad was now spooning cocoa into his mug and mine. I always had the same mug. It was a bone china one decorated with humming birds. Dad always made me cocoa before I went to bed, whatever the time was. One of his little rituals you might say. But it was also one of many barely significant memories that I would later cherish forever. However that night, all I wanted to do was go to bed. Go to bed and dream of Adam.

"What did he cook?"

"Spaghetti Bol...og...nese," I slurred.

"That sounds very continental," said Dad, raising his eyebrows. "Was it nice?"

"Yeah, it was delicious," I replied. "Adam's a good cook." Then for some reason I felt I needed to add, "not as good as you though, of course."

Dad smiled, as he stirred our cocoa. "There you are," he said, handing me my mug.

"Thank you, Dad. But would you mind if I took it up to bed with me? I'm feeling really rather tired now," I yawned.

"Of course I don't mind, darling."

"Night night, then," I said, as I leant forward to give Dad a peck on the cheek.

"Sleep tight."

I managed to climb the stairs without falling up them or even more miraculously, without spilling my cocoa. I didn't even bother to take my make-up off or brush my teeth. I just slipped out of my clothes and crawled into bed, whilst my cup of cocoa turned cold on the small table beside my bed.

CHAPTER SEVEN

Adam and I started to spend more and more time together, sliding quite naturally and effortlessly into a long-term relationship. We went to see Bruce Springsteen together, then Ultravox, and then Elvis Costello. We went to lots of parties. Adam knew a lot of people and had lots of friends. Everybody seemed to like him and respect him, and he always seemed to be the life and soul of any party. He was intelligent too. Faced with any argument, whether political, religious or merely mundane, Adam could eloquently disprove any hypothesis by drawing on the vast library of knowledge that was his mind. I would usually be intimidated by someone like Adam. I had a lot of thoughts, a lot of ideas, but as soon as I uttered them, none of them would sound as impressive out loud as they did in my head. But I was never intimidated by the attention and regard Adam received by just opening his mouth; that mouth that I would gaze longingly at as he spoke, the mouth I had kissed; lose myself in those beautiful eyes that he now only had for me; watch his gesticulations, yearning for his caress, those hands that now knew every inch of me.

But even then I wasn't entirely sure how serious Adam was about me until he asked me to move in with him. I said yes immediately for I wanted nothing more than to spend all my time with him. Go to bed with him every night, wake up with him every morning. Go shopping with him at the supermarket, and in the evening, cuddle up on the settee together in front of the TV. For the first few months at least, I think we probably made love every night, possibly in every room of his little house, the house we now shared. I still couldn't quite believe that someone as gorgeous as him would want me. Not that I was the first. I knew he'd had many girlfriends before me and had even lived with one of them for a while. There were still remnants of her presence in the house, things she had left behind. The potted plants, the pretty floral curtains and matching cushions in the sitting room, and the wooden elephant on the window sill. These were things Adam would never have chosen himself, I was certain of that. "Would you mind if I changed a few things in the house?" I asked one day.

"Like what?" Adam replied.

"Oh just little things, like new bedding, new curtains and cushions, bits and pieces like that."

"I suppose," said Adam. "But why bother?"

He obviously didn't understand why this was important to me. "Well," I began, pausing to take a deep breath, "I sometimes feel as though I've just stepped into Debbie's shoes." I hated saying her name out loud. I hated hearing her name, especially on his lips. Adam had told me that he loved Debbie, that they were planning to marry, but right out of the blue she had left him for another man. Adam had confided in me one night that the break-up had devastated him. He assured me he had gotten over her and that he loved me now, but I sometimes wondered if I was just second best, a consolation prize, that if she came back into his life and he had to choose, he would still choose her.

"Don't be daft!" said Adam.

"I just want to make this home our own now. It would mean a lot to me."

Adam gazed at me with a slightly quizzical look in his eyes. "Yeah, go ahead, if it means that much to you."

I was surprised at how much I enjoyed shopping for our home. I bought new bedding, new towels, new curtains and cushions, throwing all the old ones away, as I wanted to get rid of as much as I could that had been touched by *her*. I would like to have bought a new bed as Adam had no doubt shared our bed with her before me, but I couldn't afford to replace the furniture as well. Adam would not have agreed to it anyway, as one thing I had found out about him was that he was not thriftless or improvident. Compared to me, he had experienced rather a hard upbringing, therefore had not known the luxury of wastefulness. I removed the mirror above the fireplace and replaced it with a print of *The Water Lily Pond* by Monet. I was tempted to keep the wooden elephant because I actually liked it but I knew I needed to get rid of that too, so I donated it to the local charity shop.

There was one thing however that would now take pride of place. It was something I had treasured for a very long time. Something my mother had given to me just before she'd died. It was a Murano glass black cat, about six inches high. She told me it would bring me luck. I placed it in the centre of the mantel piece, above the fireplace.

Once I got the house the way I liked it, we invited Dad round for a meal. Adam cooked as usual and was the perfect host. It was quite evident that Dad was impressed, and that meant a lot to me. Dad didn't drink as he was driving. It was a time when Dad still had the car. He sold it after he had his first heart attack and never drove again. Once he retired, he reckoned it was an unnecessary expense anyway.

I proudly showed Dad around our house. "You've got it lovely," he smiled. He could see that I was happy, and I knew that made him happy. I also knew that the only thing he regretted was that Mum was no longer here to share my happiness too.

CHAPTER EIGHT

We'd been living together for about four months before I met Adam's older brother, John. He and his wife, Jennifer were visiting from London and Adam was eager to introduce me to them. I, on the other hand, felt very apprehensive about meeting them for the first time. I was never very confident about meeting new people anyway, especially when I felt that their opinion of me mattered.

Adam and I had arranged to meet John and Jennifer in the Black Swan. Their two children weren't with them as they were staying with Jennifer's mother at the time. "There they are," said Adam, pointing towards a table in the far corner where a couple were sitting alone, wearing rather stoic expressions on their faces. I felt my stomach churn. The man at the table stood up as we approached and suddenly his face became animated. "Hi there, little brother, it's good to see you!" said John. They gave one another an affectionate, brotherly hug. John's gaze then shifted to me. "So this is the lady I've been hearing so much about?" John smiled at me warmly. "I hope you're not going to break his heart like the last one?" His tone was still jovial but I sensed a trace of caution in his voice.

John resembled Adam. He was slightly taller and had the same thick black hair, but his was beginning to turn grey at the temples. He was attractive, but less so than Adam I thought. More distinguished looking really. Jennifer had sleek blonde hair that she wore in a bob. There wasn't a hair out of place, unlike my unruly shoulder length hair which was quite dry and out of condition now after the ravages of several perms. Her make-up was perfect too, not that she seemed to be wearing much as she was blessed with natural unblemished skin.

"Take a seat, Fay," said Adam, gesturing towards the empty chair opposite Jennifer, "and I'll go and get some drinks."

"I'll have a rum and coke, please," I said before Adam had a chance to ask me.

"Would you like a drink, John? Jennifer?" asked Adam. They both politely declined Adam's offer.

I sat down and immediately felt self-conscious. I had barely met them and already Adam had left me alone in their company. The bar looked busy. I prayed inwardly that he wouldn't be long. John seemed nice, but Jennifer hadn't spoken yet. She had merely given me a fleeting, seemingly sardonic smile. After a short silent pause that seemed to last forever, John pre-empted my attempt to initiate conversation. He asked me several rather mundane questions which he probably already knew the answers to, whereas Jennifer spoke very little. Even when I addressed her directly, she seemed reticent and reluctant to engage in any meaningful conversation with me, as though this would be beneath her. "Adam tells me you have two children?" I said. It was a statement rather than a question because I already knew it to be true.

"Yes, we do," replied Jennifer.

"What are their names?"

"Daniel and Christina."

"Those are nice names," I said.

Jennifer was silent again, seemingly reluctant to volunteer any further information.

My sense of relief when Adam returned with the drinks was almost audible. After that I didn't have to try too hard to think of anything to say because Adam and John chatted almost incessantly. John went to the bar next to replenish our drinks and not long after that, John and Jennifer said they had to go.

"Are you up for a game of tennis tomorrow?" asked John, as he put on his jacket. "I'd like to beat you just once before we return to London."

"Yeah sure, if we can get a court, I'll happily beat you again," Adam laughed.

Adam played a lot of sport. Sometimes I would watch. There was something quite sexy about him running about the tennis or squash court in his shorts, the sweat seeping through his t-shirt which would rise slightly as he stretched for a particularly difficult shot, revealing a tantalizing glimpse of his tanned torso. I was useless at sport myself. My hand-eye coordination was virtually non-existent, and my legs and arms were always at least two seconds behind my brain.

We decided to stay for just one more drink before leaving ourselves. Our house was only ten minutes' walk away and it was a nice summer evening, although the air had turned chilly since we first came out.

"I think my brother approves," said Adam as we walked home, with a self-satisfied grin.

"Do you think so?" I said, with a degree of scepticism in my voice. "Well he seems like a nice bloke."

"He is.....John's one person I know I can always rely on, who's always been there for me."

"You're lucky to have him." And I realised as I said this, I was slightly envious of Adam. I was an only child and had always wondered what it must be like to have a brother or sister of my own. Jayne, who I had been friends with since primary school, was probably the closest I would ever get to having a sister.

Adam placed his hand in mine. "I'm lucky to have you too," he said, gently pulling me towards him and planting a brief but tender kiss on my lips. I smiled. We then continued walking.

"I don't think Jennifer likes me though," I ventured.

"Whatever gives you that idea?"

"Oh, I don't know," I began, unsure about how I was going to qualify this statement. "She hardly spoke to me."

"She's a bit quiet, that's all," Adam offered as an explanation.

"I think they probably thought I was a bit of a come down after your previous girlfriends," I suggested.

"What are you going on about?" said Adam, making no effort to disguise his irritation.

"Well, look at me..... I'm a mess." I looked down at my shoes in shame.

"Don't be ridiculous!" berated Adam. "I don't know why you have so little self-confidence. You're gorgeous."

A small wry smile twisted the corners of my mouth.

CHAPTER NINE

I used to feel so proud to be Adam's girlfriend, so blessed. Whenever we went out together, I would constantly search other women's faces for glimpses of admiration or jealously. Once the gawky school girl, I had finally met someone who loved me for who I was. No one had ever seemed so interested in everything I had to say and I had never realised before just how much I had to say.

If only I could be his wife, then I would know for sure that he was really mine. I desperately wanted to refer to him as my husband. Boyfriend sounded too juvenile, transient and noncommittal. I began to ask him why he hadn't asked me to marry him.

"Why do you want to get married?" he would ask. "We're fine as we are, aren't we?"

"Yes we are," I'd reply, "but I would feel you were more committed if we were to marry."

"I *am* committed," Adam would reply. "I don't need a piece of paper to prove that."

"So why were you and Debbie planning to marry?"

"That was a mistake." The tone of his voice had turned cold and serious, therefore I said nothing more on the matter.

We did eventually get married though. One evening whilst we were out having a meal at our favourite Indian restaurant, Adam proposed. Well kind of. There were no romantic gestures. He didn't go down on one knee or produce an engagement ring. What he actually said was "I've been thinking....how d'you fancy getting married?" I was over the moon nevertheless.

Adam asked Brian to be his best man. Adam had known Brian practically all of his life. "He's been like a brother to me," Adam explained.

"Won't John be offended if you don't ask him to be best man?" I asked.

"No I think he'll be fine with it," said Adam. "I was Brian's best man at his wedding so I'd like to reciprocate."

I met Brian and his wife, Alison when they invited us to a party they were holding at their house one Christmas. Adam described Brian as "probably my best and oldest friend." He went on to tell me that they were at school together and had once formed a band, practicing in Brian's garage.

"What did you play?" I asked, quite interested in this new piece of information about Adam.

"Base guitar," said Adam. "Brian played lead guitar and he also sang. We even tried to write some of our own songs."

"Were you any good?" I asked, cheekily.

"No, not really," he laughed. We never played anywhere in public. "Brian was pretty good though, he had a natural talent for it."

"Does he play now?" I asked.

"No, I don't think so."

"That's a shame." I was always envious of people who seemed to have some kind of natural talent, whether it was the ability to sing, dance or play a musical instrument well. It seemed almost reprehensible to me when that natural talent was simply squandered or not appreciated.

I was not fortunate enough to possess any natural talents. Apart from writing, I suppose. Even as I child I loved writing stories and always dreamed of becoming a famous writer one day, although as I grew older I came to realise that life doesn't usually turn out the way you expect it to, and most childhood hopes and dreams simply fade with time, making way for the ordinary and predictable.

When we arrived at Brian and Alison's house, Brian greeted us at the door with great enthusiasm and warmth, and I felt immediately relaxed. As I got to know Brian, I discovered that he always presented in much the same way. Always friendly, happy to see you, never morose, or irritated, or angry. Sometimes I would wonder if there really was any other side to him, but we all wear masks, I'm sure of that. Some people are just better at preventing their masks from slipping at inopportune moments.

"Hi!" exclaimed Brian, wearing the broadest smile I had ever seen. We stepped into the hall way. "Thank you for coming. You must be Fay? It's so good to meet you." Despite Brian's over-enthusiasm, he still managed to sound perfectly sincere.

"You too." I smiled warmly.

Brian and Alison had a lovely home. I admired their real wood floor which in those days seemed almost luxurious. A large pine coffee table stood in the centre of a beautiful Persian rug in their sitting room. I also noticed that a string of white lights and a collection of hand-crafted ornaments tastefully adorned their Christmas tree, which was real, not artificial, unlike the one that now stood almost apologetically in our little house. I made a mental note to buy a real tree next year and some new decorations to replace the tinsel and baubles that currently bedecked our house, but now seemed rather cheap and gaudy in comparison.

Brian probably spent more time chatting to Adam than he did anyone else at the party, so it was evident that they were the best of friends. They reminisced about their school days and previous exploits, mostly for my benefit I felt. By the time we left, we had all drunk rather a lot. Brian and Alison hugged us both. "Thank you for a lovely evening," I said, noticing my voice sounding slightly slurred.

"Glad you enjoyed yourself," said Alison, smiling. "Mind how you go, it's very dark outside. I'm afraid our outside light isn't working." Despite her warning, I still managed to stumble over the rockery, scraping my shin badly."

"Are you okay?" Alison called out with concern in her voice.

"Yeah, I'm fine!" I called back, between slightly gritted teeth. It really hurt but for some reason, I was too embarrassed to admit it. As I hobbled away, I could feel the blood seeping through my jeans.

CHAPTER TEN~~TEN~~

We had a modest wedding. Neither of us wanted or could afford a big wedding. We never expected anyone else to pay for it either, as neither of us were traditionalistic and were proud to be unconventional. However, after a great deal of persuasion, we yielded to my father's tenacity and accepted his offer to pay for the reception. After a simple ceremony in the local register office, we had an afternoon reception in the function room of a nearby country pub. It was a simple buffet. Jayne, who was super talented, made and decorated our wedding cake as a present to us, and Mike (who just happened to be almost as good a photographer as he was a journalist) took the photographs, most of which weren't posed because we wanted them to reflect the informality and excitement of the day. It was in fact at our wedding that Jayne and Mike were first introduced.

I wore a pretty Laura Ashley dress, mid-calf length, with a sweetheart neckline and short slightly puffed sleeves. It was embellished with hundreds of tiny blue flowers. It fitted me perfectly, gently clinging to my slim waist and draping softly from my hips. I wore a pair of blue court shoes to match, and for the finishing touches, a string of fresh-water pearls around my neck with matching earrings. Adam looked so unbelievably handsome in his dark two piece suit, white shirt and red tie.

It was a sunny day in May, barely a cloud in the sky. It was so warm that the doors of the function room were thrown open, allowing the reception party to spill out into the beautiful landscaped gardens.

Then around six o'clock a local three piece band began setting up in one corner of the function room, just as many of the guests began to wander back inside. The remains of the buffet had been cleared away and a space made in one section of the room for people to dance. As we slowly walked hand in hand into the centre of the dance floor, a circle of people began forming around us. I closed my eyes as I melted into Adam's arms, allowing him, the music and the wine to carry me away and up into the stars.

The party was still going on when we began to bid our goodbyes. "Thank you for coming," I said, just as John leant forward to give me an affectionate kiss on the cheek. And then, rather formally I thought, he shook Adam's hand. "Congratulations, little brother".

"Thanks," said Adam, leaning forward to rather awkwardly hug John with his free left arm.

Jennifer gave Adam a kiss and then to my surprise, hugged me. This display of affection rather took me aback. "You look lovely," she said, smiling. "I hope you've had a lovely day."

Suddenly I saw a different side to Jennifer; a warm and tender side. "Thank you, I have," I said, smiling warmly.

At the time, Adam and I couldn't afford a honeymoon but as a gift, John and Jennifer had generously booked a room in a posh hotel for our wedding night. We planned to have a late dinner and a few drinks in the restaurant, before we retired to our room. By the time we ate I was feeling quite hungry as we hadn't eaten since the buffet around lunchtime, and even then I had eaten very little. We both ordered steak which was a rare treat. Adam ordered a bottle of red wine from which I had only one glass. I had already had enough to drink that afternoon. Adam managed to polish off the rest though. A string quartet was positioned unobtrusively in the corner of the large room, providing chamber music for the diners and contributing to the ambience of the restaurant. A votive candle flickered within its glass holder in the centre of each table which was covered with a deep red coloured tablecloth. I noticed that the matching napkins were also made of cloth rather than paper and even had the name of the hotel monogrammed in one corner of each napkin. *Pure class* I thought, smiling to myself.

After our meal, we retired to our room. I gasped as we entered. The lighting was already subdued, the lamps at each side of the impressive four poster bed emitting a soft warm glow through their red shades. On each pillow a chocolate wrapped in gold foil and a single red rose was placed. Adam turned on the TV which stood on a chest of drawers against the wall facing the bed. "I'm just going to the bathroom," I said, with my overnight bag in my hand.

Whilst I was in the bathroom, I changed into the baby-doll nightdress with matching underwear I had secretly bought. I smiled knowingly at myself in the mirror as I knew that these wouldn't stay on my body for long. I cleaned my teeth, touched up my make-up, fluffed up my hair and sprayed myself liberally with perfume. Although we had been living together for several years, I wanted this night to be special and romantic. It would be the perfect end to a perfect day.

When I came out of the bathroom, I found Adam lying flat on his back diagonally across the bed, his feet hanging over the edge. He had taken his shoes and jacket off, but otherwise he was fully clothed. He was snoring. My face dropped with disappointment. I went over to him and shook him, which had no effect. Placing both hands on him, I shook him again but more vigorously this time. "Adam!" I shouted in his ear. The rhythm of his snoring was interrupted by a loud snort and a groan, but I could not rouse him. Tears pricked my eyes. It was typical of him to drink far too much and spoil everything! I took a deep breath and swallowed hard in an attempt to hold back the flood of tears. I was determined not to let this ruin an otherwise lovely day. I filled the little kettle on the tray which was placed on a table in the corner of the room, and proceeded to make myself a cup of coffee. I then pushed Adam onto his side so that I could lie on the bed, and removed the rose and chocolate from the pillow. I sat on the bed with my legs stretched out in front of me, placing the pillow behind my head against the headboard. I carefully unwrapped the chocolate, and as I bit into it, its liqueur centre escaped into my mouth. *Yummy, this is quite delicious* I thought. I had a sip of my coffee which was still rather hot, then reached for the chocolate on Adam's pillow. I glowered at Adam and ate his chocolate too, with as much relish as the first. I turned off the TV. There was nothing on worth watching. I wished now that I had brought a book or a magazine to read, but then I didn't think I would need one. I yawned. I was actually more tired than I thought. So I slipped under the covers and before long, my thoughts began to wander and I was fast asleep.

CHAPTER ELEVEN

When I woke, Adam was in bed, lying on his side with his back facing me. He had obviously got undressed during the night because the rest of his clothes were lying across the chair in the corner of the room and he was naked. I gently stroked his black wavy hair. He murmured then turned around to face me. He draped his arm across me and was smiling, his eyes still closed.

"Would you like a cuppa?" I asked.

"Yes please," he said, sleepily, still not opening his eyes.

I slid out from underneath his embrace and out of bed. I filled the kettle and switched it on. I then went into the bathroom. I caught sight of myself in the mirror. I hadn't taken my make-up off the night before. My mascara was smudged but otherwise I looked reasonably human. When I came back from the bathroom, Adam was half-sitting up in bed, with one arm folded behind his head. "I haven't seen that before.....it's very sexy," he said, grinning.

I looked down at the baby-doll nightdress I was wearing. "I bought it specially....for last night...except you fell asleep." There was a tinge of disappointment in my voice.

"I'm sorry. I was really tired. Perhaps we could make up for it now?"

"I need a cup of tea first," I said.

"That can wait can't it?"

"You should know me by now," I said. "I'm not really a morning person. What I want most when I first wake up is a cup of tea. Everything else has to wait for at least half an hour."

"What time do we have to be out of our room?" Adam asked.

"I think it's ten," I said, picking up my watch to check the time. "It's only quarter to eight now."

“Okay, have your cup of tea,” he acquiesced. “Could you make mine a coffee?”

I nodded as I began to tear open the sachets of sugar and empty them into the cups. Adam threw back the quilt, stood up and made his way across the room towards the bathroom. He was totally naked which wasn’t unusual. That was how he always slept. I turned my head slightly to watch him walk. He still had a good body and felt totally at ease walking around naked, whereas I would still find myself shrinking with embarrassment whenever Adam saw me totally naked in unsubdued light, despite how long I’d known him.

I was sat up in bed still drinking my tea when Adam began gently caressing my arm. “That tickles,” I chuckled. “And I’m trying to drink my tea.”

“Put the cup down now, Fay. I can’t resist you any longer I’m afraid.” Adam’s tone was gently teasing. I did as I was told, shuffling down the bed and turning to face Adam, who was smiling seductively at me. *My God,* I thought, *he’s still as sexy as he ever was…….*

CHAPTER TWELVE

Less than a year after we married, I found out I was pregnant. It wasn't a complete surprise. We weren't actually 'trying for a baby'. That has always seemed an odd statement to me, like you have to put in some sort of effort and practice to get it right. I just stopped taking the pill and we waited to see what would happen. I got pregnant pretty quickly. We were still having sex fairly regularly then. Apart from the times I felt ill, I quite enjoyed being pregnant and as my bump gradually swelled, so did my pride. In fact, ironically, I think it was the first time I felt truly beautiful. Towards the end however, I felt very uncomfortable and had difficulty sleeping, particularly as the baby would start hiccupping late at night...a strange sensation really but reassuring all the same. When I finally went into labour I was relieved, even though the baby was almost a week early.

No one can really prepare you for the experience of giving birth. All the breathing exercises I had learnt went straight out the window. I remember saying to Adam, "this is the worst pain I have ever felt. I'm *never* going through this again." Despite my initial reservations, I yielded to the promise of an end to the pain. The Midwife injected Pethidine into my thigh and almost immediately I felt the drug taking effect as I began to swiftly slip away. Then another contraction, not as intense as before, but enough to wake me from my slumber. As the hours went by, I grew more and more tired. As the pain of each contraction reached a crescendo, I'd hear the midwife's soothing voice, "you're doing really well, just one more push."

"I can't," I complained, exhausted, "I'm too tired."

"You're nearly there," she encouraged. But she'd been saying that for the past two hours. The midwife *was* wonderful, and so was Adam, as he stayed by my side, his hand clasped tightly in mine throughout, although I don't think I would have cared less if the entire Queen's Guard Regiment had also been in the delivery room with us, for any sense of embarrassment I expected to feel flew straight out of the window too.

When our baby was finally delivered, I vaguely remember hearing the midwife announce, "it's a boy." Wrapped in a towel she handed him to me and I remember seeing his beautiful screwed up little face for the first time. What I don't remember immediately feeling is the overwhelming love and joy I expected to feel, probably because I was so tired and nauseas, I think I was just glad it was all over. "What are you going to call him?" she asked. Adam and I looked at each other and smiled. "Ben," I said.

By the time I fell asleep to the first song of the skylark, it must have been around four in the morning. I awoke when I heard Ben being wheeled in his portable cot onto the ward and then parked alongside my bed. He had been taken to the nursery once I returned to the ward so that I could get some sleep. Ben was quiet now and I assumed he was sleeping, so I allowed myself to drift back off to sleep also.

Adam didn't return until the afternoon by which time I felt desperate to see him. I was lying on the bed, holding Ben in my arms, when Adam walked through the door holding a huge teddy bear and a box of chocolates.

"Hi, Darling," said Adam, planting a tender kiss on my lips. "How are you feeling?"

"Fine really. Just tired."

"Did you manage to get some sleep?"

"Some."

Adam placed the chocolates on the bedside cupboard, although the last thing I felt like eating was chocolates. He then placed the teddy bear at the foot of the bed. We then decided to nestle Ben in between the teddy's paws, so that we could take a photo. The teddy was at least three times the size of Ben. Already I was beginning to feel a bond, a bond that would never be broken. I began to love Ben more than I could have ever imagined before. I understood for the first time the real meaning of a mother's love. I knew that I would do anything to protect him, that I would gladly die for him. Any love I had experienced before he was born could not compare with the love I felt for him then.

∞

I turned on the bedside lamp and lifted Ben out of his carry cot. He was now eight weeks old and already getting heavier. After I had fed him, and he lay in my arms sleeping, I could just feel the delicate movements of his tiny silent breaths. Adam then woke. "Hi," he said, sleepily. Then propping himself up on his elbow, he leaned over to kiss Ben tenderly on his head.

"He's just beautiful, isn't he?" I whispered, smiling.

"And so are you," Adam whispered back. As I turned my head towards him, he planted a gentle kiss on my lips. Then Adam lay his head back on his pillow and draped his arm around me and over mine, so both our arms were cradling Ben.

We were a family, a beautiful family. And I tried to cling to that one fleeting moment of happiness, untainted by any pain or regrets that may follow, because I wanted it to last forever. And I wanted to always remember how I felt at that moment, when life was so full of hope. No matter what happened in years to come, I knew that I would always be happy at that one precise and perfect moment in time.

CHAPTER THIRTEEN

I went back to work when Ben was only four months old. When I wasn't at work, a lot of my time was devoted to Ben. I always felt a bit guilty about returning to work so soon, so I would try to give Ben as much quality time as I could, often over-compensating by spoiling him with toys and expensive outings. Looking back I now realise that Adam, Ben and I never did much together as a family. It was usually just me and Ben.

"I'm thinking about taking Ben to the Safari park this Saturday," I suggested to Adam one day. I think Ben was about eight or nine years old at the time. "Whilst the weather's so good. I thought he could invite his friend, Richard. There's also a fair there and a sea lion show. They'll love that."

"Yeah, that sounds good," said Adam, absentmindedly, making little effort to feign interest or enthusiasm.

"I thought it might be nice if you came too," I suggested somewhat tentatively. "It's been a while since we did anything together as a family. We could take a picnic. The weather forecast is good."

"Is there a bar there?" Adam teased; although I sensed he wasn't joking; so I threw him a black look. Then to my surprise, he added, "okay, I'll come." I expected him to require a little more persuasion.

Three days later I was packing the picnic basket for our day out. It was only 9.00 in the morning but the sun was already high in the sky. It was unusually warm, even for July. "Can you put these in as well," said Adam, handing me two cans of lager.

"Have you really got to take these?" I asked, impatiently. "I'm not sure there's enough room in the basket."

"Well, put them in a separate bag then."

With a heavy sigh, I rearranged the items in the basket to make room for the cans, which I just managed to fit in. "I'm assuming that you're expecting me to drive then?"

"Well it was your idea to go," said Adam. "Besides, if I wasn't coming, you'd be driving anyway." I said nothing in reply.

At 9.30 we left, collecting Ben's friend, Richard along the way. The park opened at 10.00 and I anticipated it only taking us about forty minutes to get there. The boys sat in the back of the car, chatting excitedly about which animals they were going to feed and which rides they would go on at the fair. Then Ben asked the predictable question, "are we there yet?"

"Nearly," I reassured him. Five minutes later we were queuing at the entrance to the park. "Two adults and two children please. Oh, and could I have a guide book and two packets of animal feed?" The lady in the booth handed me the tickets, book and packets of animal feed as I stretched my arm out of the open window of the car to hand her the money.

We followed the slow moving line of traffic around the winding road of the park. I allowed the boys to take their seat belts off so that they could kneel on the back seat to look out of the windows. It was stiflingly warm as the car had no air conditioning, and during certain sections of the park we had to keep the windows closed. I think we were all relieved when we could park the car and make our way to the picnic area. We spotted a vacant table and benches. I took out the antiseptic hand wipes first and instructed the boys to wipe their hands. I then emptied the contents of the picnic basket on to the table and Adam claimed his cans of lager. "I bet they're a bit warm aren't they?" I said.

"Yeah, they are a bit," said Adam. "We could have done with a cool bag".

The boys ate ravenously. It had been a long time since breakfast.

After our picnic, we made our way to the pets' corner where the boys could stroke some of the gentler animals up close. It also gave me the opportunity to take some more photos, little mementos of our special day out. I think even then I knew that these moments were precious and needed to be cherished.

We then made our way to the fair, checking the schedule for the sea lion show along the way. There was a show already in progress so we agreed to attend the next one which was at three o'clock. We then stood in the queue to buy wristbands for the rides. As soon as the boys had their bands fastened securely around their wrists, they ran off excitedly, in two different directions. "Wait!" I called out. "Don't run off!" They obediently stopped and waited for me and Adam to catch up. "I hope they're not sick, going on the rides so soon after their lunch," I said to Adam, seeking some reassurance.

“No, I’m sure they’ll be fine.”

After the boys had a ride on just about everything in the park, I said “one more ride and then we need to make our way to the sea lions if we want to see the show.” After their ride, I bought the boys an ice lolly each to quench their thirst, and then we took our places in the queue.

“You don’t mind if I don’t come in, do you?” asked Adam.

Bewildered, I replied, “what are you going to do while we’re in there?”

“I thought I’d pop to the bar.”

“I’m not sure that there is one,” I said, knowing full well there was because I had spotted it on our way from the picnic area.

“Yeah, there is.”

I frowned. “I suppose I don’t mind.” I suddenly felt very irritated, although I didn’t really know why.

CHAPTER FOURTEEN

We were driving back from the safari park and the boys were playing with the toy animals they had acquired during our visit to the gift shop, when Ben asked suddenly "can Richard come back to play?"

"Not now," I said.

"Why?" whined Ben.

"His mum will be expecting him home," I explained. "Maybe he could come for tea one evening after school?" I glanced in the rear view mirror and noticed Ben's frown turn into a smile.

"Yeah! Can he?" asked Ben, excitedly.

"If he wants to," I replied. "And if his mum says he can."

After I had dropped Richard off at home and made arrangements with his mother about him coming for tea after school the following Tuesday, Adam said "would you mind taking a slight detour to drop me off in town?"

"Why?"

"I thought I'd pop into the Queen's Head for a quick drink."

"No, I suppose not," I sighed.

"Thanks," said Adam, as he climbed out of the car a few minutes later. "I won't be long."

Four hours later I heard Adam fumbling with his keys, in an attempt to open the front door. I rose from the settee to let him in. "Thanks. I couldn't find the right key in the dark." I walked back through to the sitting room, resuming my position on the settee. "What are you watching?" I then noticed his speech was slurred.

"Just a documentary," I said. "It's really rather interesting." Then with my eyes still fixed on the television, I said "there's a message on the answerphone for you from Brian. He wants to know if you want a game of squash with him tomorrow."

"I'll give him a ring," said Adam, picking up the telephone receiver at the foot of the stairs.

"Don't you think it's a bit late?"

"No, he won't mind."

I continued to watch the documentary, whilst eaves dropping on the conversation Adam was having with Brian. I heard him making some excuse for not being able to play squash the following day.

"Why didn't you want a game?" I asked, after Adam replaced the receiver.

"To be honest, I've lost interest in squash."

"You never seem to play any sport now," I said, with some concern in my voice.

"So? What's your point?" said Adam, somewhat defensively.

"Well," I began, tentatively, "you could do with losing a few pounds." My gaze shifted from his face to his beer belly.

"That's the pot calling the kettle black, isn't it?" And with that remark, I looked down, placing the palm of my hand on my tummy, in a vain attempt to conceal my own slight paunch. I briefly entertained the idea of suggesting we start exercising together, but quickly dismissed it.

"I know," I conceded. "I just think it's a shame, that's all. I have never been into sport myself, but it used to be an important part of your life, once upon a time." It was true; Adam used to play some kind of sport, whether it be tennis, squash or badminton, at least two or three times a week. He used to be slim, fit and sexy. But recently I had noticed he'd put on rather a lot of weight. Adam wasn't much taller than me, so it didn't really suit him at all. I was beginning to worry that I didn't find him as attractive as I used to.

"Well I'm going to bed now," said Adam. "Are you coming?"

"I'm just going to finish watching this, then I'll be up."

"Okay."

By the time I slipped into bed beside Adam, he was snoring like a bull elephant seal. I lay there for a while, contemplating. At one time, we would always go to bed together and always fall asleep in each other's arms, often after making love. I could not remember the last time that had happened. I would tell myself that for most couples who had been together for as long as we had, the excitement and ardour they once felt would inevitably be replaced by the constancy of companionship. And that was really okay. That was normal. That was nice.

I shoved Adam hard, in a vain attempt to move him from his back onto his side. I then realised that I would probably spend half the night awake if I stayed where I was, so I decided to get up before I got too comfortable. I grabbed my pillow and the spare duvet from the top of the wardrobe and went downstairs to sleep on the settee, cursing Adam under my breath as I went.

CHAPTER FIFTEEN

The next morning, the pleasing sound of a child's laughter penetrated my dreams. I opened my eyes to see Ben sat on the arm chair adjacent to me, still in his pyjamas, staring almost unblinkingly at the television. I groaned as I tried to sit up, for I felt stiff and ached all over. Ben glanced in my direction, then without a word, fixed his gaze back on the television. "Good morning, Ben," I said, sleepily.

"Good morning, mummy. Why are you sleeping on the settee?"

"Daddy was snoring," I explained.

Just then, as though he were taking his cue, Adam entered the room with a mug of tea in his hand which he placed on the coffee table in front of me.

"Thank you," I said.

"I'm sorry. Was I snoring again?"

"Yes," I replied, rather grumpily. "My back's killing me."

"Let me make it up to you," said Adam. "Why don't we go out for lunch today?"

"Where shall we go?"

"How about *The Shakespeare*? They do a really nice carvery there."

"Okay," I replied. "Do we need to book?"

"It would probably be a good idea. Say for about 1.00?"

"Okay, that'll be nice," I smiled, and he was instantly forgiven.

∞

It was a quarter to twelve and I'd just got out the shower. "I'm just popping out for a drink!" Adam called from the bottom of the stairs.

I put on my robe and began padding down the stairs towards him. "I thought we were going for a meal?"

"We are. I won't be long. I'm just going for a quick drink with the lads."

I gave him a scrutinizing look. "You *will* be back by quarter to one at the latest, won't you?"

"Of course I will." And then he left.

∞

It was a quarter to one and Adam wasn't back yet. I was starting to feel irritated, but then said to myself, *just give him a few more minutes, I'm sure he's on his way*.

It was now one o'clock and I was fuming. I'd just telephoned the Black Horse but Adam wasn't there. Short of ringing round every pub, I had no way of contacting him. In those days, Adam didn't possess a mobile phone. I busied myself by checking my hair and re-applying my lipstick in the mirror in the hallway.

"When are we going?" whined Ben. "I'm hungry."

"We're just waiting for Daddy. I'm sure he won't be long."

It was now ten minutes past one. *Right, we'll wait five more minutes and if Adam's not here by then, we'll go without him,* I told myself.

It was quarter past one. "Right, Ben, time to go," I said, standing up suddenly.

"What about Daddy?"

"Well he's obviously got held up somewhere, so I think we should go without him. He'll probably meet us there."

When we arrived at *The Shakespeare* we were half an hour late for our table. When we sat down with our plates laden with meat, Yorkshire pudding and vegetables, I glanced around and noticed that all of the other tables were occupied by couples or families. I suddenly felt so conspicuous. I smiled and chatted merrily with Ben, so that no one would suspect we were alone not by choice, whilst underneath I was secretly seething.

When we arrived back home later that afternoon, we found Adam sprawled out on the settee, snoring as usual. I made a mental note not to forgive him this time, not for a very long time at least.

I went to bed early that night. In fact, as soon as I had got Ben bathed and settled. I was feeling really tired due to my disturbed sleep the night before, and was now beginning to feel a bit queasy. Adam was still asleep on the settee. He had woken up briefly a couple of times but I had chosen to ignore him.

CHAPTER SIXTEEN

I must have fallen asleep almost straight away as before I knew it, an incessant high-pitched alarm infiltrated my dreams. Frantically I tried to subdue the almost unbearable clangour of the clock, even to the point that I threw it out of the window. Nevertheless, it would not stop. I plugged my ears with my fingers but still the deafening noise rang in my head. Then I woke up and clumsily reached out for the clock which was still on the bedside table. I looked at the time. I needed to get up but I still felt somewhat nauseous. The nausea quickly built up in my stomach, then up into my throat. I knew I needed to vomit but I didn't want to. I hated being sick. I stayed in bed for as long as I could, wrapped up in my duvet, not daring to move, trying to suppress the need to vomit for as long as I could.

Eventually I jumped out of bed and rushed to the bathroom where I was unceremoniously sick in the toilet, a mixture of pine toilet cleaner and vomit hitting my senses. I knelt down on the cold linoleum floor, placing my head in my hands. God, I felt *so* ill. Eventually I staggered back to bed, when I was fairly sure I wasn't going to be sick again. "Adam," I said, "I'm really ill. Can you make sure Ben gets ready for school and give him his breakfast, then drop him off at school on your way to work please?"

I've got to get ready myself," said Adam, "but if you can get him ready, I'll drop him off at school."

I felt too tired and ill to argue, so I dragged my languid body back out of bed and shuffled into Ben's bedroom. "Ben! It's time to get up," I said, barely opening my eyes. "Come on!"

Eventually Ben got out of bed. "I'm not feeling very well today, Ben. So try and be good for me, won't you? Go and wash your hands and face and clean your teeth, then get dressed and comb your hair, as quick as you can. I'll go downstairs and start to make your breakfast. Daddy's going to give you a lift to school today so you can't keep him waiting."

As soon as Adam and Ben were out the front door and I had waved Ben good-bye with a forced smile on my face, I rang my office to report I was sick. I then poured myself a glass of water and went back to bed. Relieved, I knew I wouldn't have to pick Ben up from school as Jayne always did that, when she collected her own daughter, Sarah who was round about the same age as Ben.

I had the following day off work as well, returning to work on the Wednesday. I hadn't forgotten about Adam letting me and Ben down on the Sunday, but the event had shrunk in significance whilst I was throwing my guts up in the toilet. It was still there though, stored in the recesses of my mind, to be dragged out when required as evidence in future arguments. I was thankful that Ben had not been ill also, but that night Adam started complaining of feeling unwell himself. "I think I might be coming down with what you had," he said. By the following morning, he was being sick in the bathroom. It obviously wasn't the carvery dinner that had made me ill as Adam hadn't eaten any.

When I arrived home from work, after picking Ben up from Jayne's, Adam was still in bed. "How are you feeling?"

"I feel terrible," he groaned. He had the duvet pulled up to his neck and he was shivering. His face was glistening with sweat. I touched his forehead.

"You're cold," I said, drawing my hand away in surprise. "Do you want anything to eat or drink?"

"I don't think I'd be able to keep anything down," said Adam. "Perhaps just some water."

I went back downstairs and poured Adam a glass of water. "There you are," I said, placing the glass on the bedside table next to Adam. "Do you think you need a doctor?"

"No, I don't think that's necessary," he said, with a shaky voice.

Adam didn't really get up until the next day. He still had no appetite and complained of feeling very weak, but he was beginning to look a little better. Or was that because he hadn't had a drink for a couple of days?

∞

"Fay!" Somebody was whispering my name but with a sense of urgency in their voice. Then I felt their hand on me, shaking me. I woke to find Adam looking down on me, his wide eyes shining in the semi-darkness.

"What is it?" I asked, sitting up and switching on my bedside lamp.

"I'm scared," he said, with a genuine sense of fear in his voice.

I looked at my alarm clock. “It’s only four o’clock in the morning. What are you frightened of?”

“I can’t see them now, now that you’ve turned the light on.”

“See what?”

“Faces. Horrible faces….looming over me….in the dark.”

I sighed. I was concerned, but even more so, I was tired. ”It was just a bad dream,” I assured him, as though I was comforting a small child.

“No, it wasn’t, because I wasn’t asleep,” said Adam.

“I’ll leave the light on. Lie down next to me.” And with that, I put my arm around him, resting my head on his chest. I could feel the heat radiating from his body and hear his heart pounding in my ear.

CHAPTER SEVENTEEN

By the following evening, Adam was starting to feel a lot better. He hadn't had an alcoholic drink for about three days. Probably the longest he had gone without a drink for a very long time.

"Why don't you stay off the drink for a while?" I suggested. "I think it will do you good to give your body a break." I had been starting to worry quite a bit about the amount Adam was drinking. Admittedly, Adam had always enjoyed a drink and there seemed to be nothing particularly unusual about that. But it had become more than that. It was as if he *needed* it now.

"Yeah, you're probably right," said Adam.

But by the following evening, he was back in the pub, after returning to work that day. I was disappointed, but was reluctant to take on the role of a nagging wife, so said nothing. That had recently become a habit, going for a drink straight after work, "a chance to unwind," as he put it. Sometimes he didn't come home until seven or eight in the evening.

It was now almost nine o'clock and Ben was in bed watching a video. Adam still wasn't home, so I decided to make myself something to eat. I placed a large potato in the microwave and while that was cooking, grated some cheese onto a plate, adding some coleslaw and three cherry tomatoes. *Adam will have to get himself something to eat when he comes home*, I thought to myself.

It was now almost ten o'clock and I was beginning to wonder whether or not I should be ringing round hospitals when Adam arrived home. "Sorry I'm so late," he said, as he entered the living room where I was still seated.

"I was beginning to worry."

"It's just that," faltered Adam, "I've had some bad news at work today."

"Oh?"

"They announced the redundancies," said Adam, sitting down next to me.

"I thought you said your job was safe."

"Apparently I was wrong."

"Oh…." I looked at Adam who now had his head in his hands. I didn't really know what to say. "I'm sure you'll get another job."

"Well at least I'll get a decent redundancy package," said Adam. "I thought I'd give Brian a ring to see if there are any vacancies at his place."

∞

But there were no vacancies at Brian's company. So Adam began to look elsewhere. However his search for a new job was in vain. In fact, as time went by, the less motivated Adam became and the more he seemed to drink.

I had arrived home after a particularly gruelling day at work. I walked in to find Adam sprawled out on the settee, snoring with his mouth agape. There were a couple of cans of beer on the coffee table, one empty and one half full. Then panic set in.

Adam had agreed to pick Ben up from school that day. Jayne was away on holiday, so she hadn't been able to collect Ben from school all that week or look after him until I finished work. I had taken three days off work at the beginning of the week, so Adam only had to pick Ben up from school on the Thursday and on the Friday. Several times I had impressed upon Adam how important it was not to forget to pick Ben up. He was only nine years old and although Ben would insist he was big enough now to walk home by himself, I wasn't ready to let that happen yet. At least *not until big school* as I had explained to Ben on more than one occasion.

I slipped off my sandals and headed upstairs, my breath quickening. "Ben!" I called out.

"Yeah!" Ben called back, and I exhaled a heavy sigh of relief. Ben was in his bedroom playing with his toys on the floor.

"Did Daddy pick you up from school?" I asked.

"No," replied Ben, still engrossed in his game. "I walked home by myself." He looked up now and smiled broadly at me, showing off the gap in his front teeth."

"Was Daddy here when you got home?" I asked, trying not to betray any anxiety in my voice.

"Yeah," said Ben, unconcerned, "but he was asleep."

"How did you get in?"

"I got the spare key from under the flower pot."

Part of me was proud of how resourceful Ben had been, but a bigger part of me was furious with Adam for being so irresponsible.

CHAPTER EIGHTEEN

The following morning, I could feel Adam who was still in bed, watching me whilst I was getting ready for work. “Are you okay?” he asked. “You seem very quiet this morning.”

I glared at Adam, without saying a word. He was half-sitting up in bed, his arms folded behind his head.

“What’s wrong?” Adam asked, innocently. “I apologised last night for forgetting to pick Ben up, and I thought you’d accepted my apology.”

“We need to talk,” I stated, my tone devoid of all emotion.

“Oh dear, that sounds ominous,” he said, with a wry smile. “What d’you want to talk about?”

“Our situation.”

“What about our situation?”

“I haven’t got time to talk now, I need to get to work. Tonight.....when I get back....we’ll talk then. Just make sure you don’t forget to pick Ben up from school today.”

“Don’t worry, I won’t,” Adam assured me.

I threw Adam a look that indicated I was not reassured by his words one little bit. “See you later,” I said, coldly, picking up my bag and flouncing out the door.

∞

As I drove home from work that evening, I began to prepare an imaginary conversation in my head, a conversation that involved me eloquently expressing my point of view and suggesting ways in which we could improve our situation, and Adam listening without interruption, and then agreeing with everything I said.

As I turned the key in the front door, I half-expected to hear resounding snores from the sitting room, but as I entered the house, I was greeted with a smile and an offer of a cup of tea.

"Yes, please," I said, as Adam disappeared into the kitchen. I kicked off my shoes and sat down on the settee with a sigh. I felt exhausted after another busy day at work, almost too tired now to have *the talk* I knew we needed to have.

Adam emerged from the kitchen with my tea, placing it on the coaster on the coffee table before me. He then sat down beside me on the settee.

"Thanks."

"So what is it you want to talk about?" asked Adam. "I've been on tenterhooks all day."

"Where's Ben?"

"He's playing upstairs," said Adam. "Well?"

"You really have no idea, have you?"

"No, I'm afraid I don't." Adam seemed genuinely perplexed. "I know I forgot to pick Ben up from school and I'm extremely sorry about that."

I emitted a deep sigh in preparation for the speech I had prepared earlier. "It's not just that.....although that was bad enough. I'm very unhappy about our current situation," I began.

"Well so am I, but I didn't ask to be made redundant, did I?" said Adam, defensively.

"I know....I know it's not your fault you were made redundant but I'd have a bit more respect for you if you were making a little more effort to look for another job. Instead you seem to be spending all day every day getting pissed, spending money on booze we can't really afford. You do nothing to help me around the house...."

"I've just made you a cup of tea, haven't I?"

"Well, whoopee do!" I retorted sarcastically.

"Look, what's this really all about? Have you got another fella? I'd rather you just told me."

"That's just typical of you! The fact that I'm not happy can't possibly be your fault, so it must be down to the fact that I've got someone else."

"Well, have you?"

"No," I said, emphatically. "But I'm starting to get really worried about our relationship. I feel that we're drifting apart and I don't want that to happen." My tone was softer now.

"Well neither do I." Adam reached out for my hand. I acquiesced by placing my hand in his.

“I’m prepared to try harder if you are. I will promise to try to stop nagging you if you would agree to try to cut down your drinking.”

“Of course, I can do that,” said Adam, squeezing my hand. “I know my drinking has got a bit out of control recently, but that can change.....from now.”

CHAPTER NINETEEN

Adam did eventually get another job in the Customer Services department of a large online company. It was a step down from his previous position of Senior Planner and was less money. But it was a job. For a while Adam seemed much more in control. He was still drinking but seemed to be functioning perfectly well. After nearly twelve months, we had managed to put some money away and could afford to book a holiday. Ben was now ten years old and we hadn't been abroad since he was a toddler.

I was on my way home with an armful of holiday brochures ready to spend the afternoon searching for our ideal holiday. Adam had taken Ben to the local pitch and put which was a rare treat for Ben, and a rare experience for Adam, spending quality father and son time together. By the time they arrived home later that afternoon, I had chosen our holiday. I just needed Adam and Ben to agree with my choice.

"I think this is just what we're looking for," I said, excitedly, opening one of the brochures at the page I had folded over earlier. "We can go all inclusive, which means we won't need much spending money. It's got two swimming pools and lots of facilities, including a kids club. It's close to the beach, which looks lovely by the way."

"Sounds great," said Adam. "Where is it? And more importantly, how much is it?"

"It's in Majorca," I said. "And it's really very reasonable."

"Can I see?" said Ben, landing with a bounce next to me on the settee. I showed Ben the pictures in the brochure which, most importantly, met with his approval.

So the decision was made.

∞

Six months later we were on a plane to Palma airport. We allowed Ben to have the window seat so he could get a good view. Fortunately, It was a daytime flight. "Wow!" Ben exclaimed. "We're higher than the clouds!"

I smiled. I was so glad Ben was old enough now to appreciate things like that. "Do you want a drink, Ben?" I asked. "They're coming round with the drinks trolley now."

"Yeah, can I have orange juice please, Mum?"

"Of course you can, Darling." So I ordered an orange juice for Ben, and also one for myself. "What about you, Adam?"

"I'll have two bottles of red wine and a can of beer, please," said Adam. I glared at him as the stewardess handed Adam his drinks.

"Did you have to order *all* those drinks?"

"Each bottle's only equivalent to a glass, and the beer's not even half a pint," said Adam. "Besides, they might not be coming round again with the drinks."

"It's just embarrassing that's all. It's barely lunchtime and we're not even going to be on the plane that long."

"Look, if you're going to nag me like this for the rest of the holiday....." began Adam, slightly raising his voice.

"No, I won't," I interjected. "I'm sorry, I'll try to lighten up." But already I could feel my stomach churning. *Perhaps I should just get drunk myself*, I thought. *At least then I might not even care.*

As we stepped off the plane and descended the steps onto the runway, the heat hit us, dry and unruffled by even the slightest breeze. I reached in my handbag for my sunglasses. It was mid-afternoon and the sun was high in the sky.

We seemed to be waiting forever beside the carousel for our luggage. Then there was the coach journey, stopping at almost every hotel it seemed before we reached our destination. By the time it was our turn to leave the coach and wheel our cases up towards the entrance to our hotel, we all felt tired, hot and cranky. "I'm going to jump straight into the pool!" announced Ben.

"We need to check into our room first, Ben," I said.

"But I'm too hot!" whined Ben.

"It won't take long," I assured him. "Besides, you need to change into your trunks first if you want to go swimming."

It was a lovely room. Simple but immaculate and tastefully decorated with pale wooden furniture and a parquet tiled floor. It had a double bed, and a single bed for Ben, with matching cream coloured bedding. On the balcony, which overlooked the pool, stood a small cast metal table and chairs painted white. We had barely got into the room when Ben was already stripping off his clothes. "Where's my trunks?" he asked, impatiently, starting to unzip one of the bags.

"They're not in there, Ben," I said. "Your clothes are in this bag." I began to unzip the bag. Then Ben was there, frantically pulling his clothes out, in search of his trunks. "Just wait, Ben," I chided. "You're messing all your clothes up. I'll get them out for you." A minute later he was wearing his trunks and was heading out the door. "Wait, Ben! You're not to go down to the pool by yourself. You don't even know the way. Just sit on the bed and wait for us, please."

"Oh, Mom!" whined Ben, petulantly, plonking himself down on the edge of the bed, his sandalled feet only just reaching the floor.

"I can take him down to the pool if you're not ready," suggested Adam.

"Okay, if you don't mind." Ben was already on his feet and heading towards the door. "Let me just give you a towel for Ben," I said, unzipping one of the cases.

"Do you think you'll be able to find us okay?" asked Adam.

"Yeah, I'm sure I will," I replied. "See you in a little while."

I welcomed the chance to freshen up and unpack. If Adam and Ben were here on their own, they probably wouldn't bother unpacking at all and would just live out of their suitcases for the entire holiday.

Approximately half an hour later, I made my way to the pool. Ben was already splashing around in the water. The pool was almost empty as evening was fast approaching. Adam was sat at a table close to the pool with a glass of beer in his hand. "Hi," said Adam. "Would you like a drink?"

"I'd love a cup of coffee," I said, sitting down at the table. Adam knocked back the rest of his drink, then walked over to the poolside bar to get another beer and a coffee for me.

∞

The following morning we dutifully attended the welcome meeting, when our holiday rep informed us of all the facilities the hotel had to offer and the over-priced excursions we could go on. Ben sat patiently, drinking his orange juice through a straw. "The kids club sounds good, Ben," I said, enthusiastically. "I thought we could spend some quality time together while Ben's there." I smiled suggestively at Adam.

"That sounds like a great idea," said Adam, squeezing my hand. He knew exactly what I meant by *quality time.* It was probably the only opportunity we would have, seeing as we were sharing a room with Ben.

∞

The following day seemed even hotter than the one before. "Ben!" I called. "You need to put your t-shirt on now, in case you burn."

"Okay, mum!" he called back, making his way to the side of the pool. He climbed out and trotted over towards me, dripping wet, looking so skinny in just his trunks.

I stretched the t-shirt over his head, and immediately he was back in the pool, giving me no time to rub in any more sun cream onto the parts of his body still exposed. Ben was already turning a lovely golden brown colour. He followed Adam in that respect, whereas all I could hope for from hours spent in the sun would be uneven patches of anything from strawberry pink to lobster red.

Later that afternoon, Ben was showered and changed ready for the kids club. After we dropped Ben off, Adam and I were back in our room with a *do not disturb* sign hanging from the handle of the door, just in case one of the maids decided to let herself in. Adam stripped off his clothes. Despite the fact that he had put on a little too much weight and his hair was now greying, he was still an attractive man, especially now that he was already sporting a deep golden tan. Adam tried to pull my top up over my head, getting it stuck on my ears. "Let me do it," I chuckled. A couple of minutes later we were lying down on the bed together, making love for the first time in months.

CHAPTER TWENTY

I should have known. Booking an all-inclusive holiday was never going to be a good idea. Not for Adam, for he was bound to want to get his money's worth. On the third day of our holiday, he exceeded my expectations. We were having our evening meal in the hotel's restaurant with Ben. We all helped ourselves to the buffet and Adam filled a picture with red wine from one of the barrels. This was his second picture that evening. He had also been drinking all day long, so I should have noticed just how drunk Adam was getting. When it was time for us to get up from the table to leave, Adam was incapable of standing without my help. Then Ben and I headed towards the open door of the restaurant, carefully weaving our way around the tables, with Adam following behind. Except Adam was bumping into tables, knocking people's drinks over as he went. "He's had a bit too much vino, hasn't he?" laughed one of the diners, a middle-aged man with his family I had seen in the restaurant every evening since we had arrived there. They even seemed to be sitting at the same table as before.

"Yeah!" I laughed back, although inside I was dying with embarrassment, wishing that a big hole would open and swallow me up.

Once we were outside the restaurant, I suggested we had an early night. "Maybe we could sit and have a drink on the balcony? Then Ben can get to bed. He had a late night last night and was up early this morning."

"But I'm not tired," whined Ben.

"Let's not go up yet," said Adam. "It's too early."

"Well you can stay out a bit longer if you like, but I'm going up with Ben."

"Oh no, Mom!" whined Ben again.

"Just do as you're told!" I snapped. "We're going up." With that I grabbed Ben's hand. Then realising I was unacceptably displacing my irritation onto Ben, with a much gentler tone, I added "I'll get us both a hot chocolate to take up and then I'll read you a story if you like." Ben's frown turned into a smile. "Say good night to Daddy."

∞

I'm not sure what time it was when Adam came to bed, but I know he woke me from a pleasant dream as he fell on top of me whilst trying to undress in the dark. "Ouch!" I shrieked, trying to push him off of me. "What the hell are you doing?" I reached out for the switch above my head and turned on one of the small lights.

"What's happening?" asked Ben, sleepily.

"It's okay," I said, in a much calmer tone. "Go back to sleep."

Unfortunately I wasn't able to go back to sleep myself, because once Adam had managed to climb into bed next to me, virtually as soon as his head hit the pillow, he began snoring loudly.

CHAPTER TWENTY-ONE

Eventually I must have fallen asleep because again I was woken from a dream, but by Ben this time, who was gently shaking me. "Mom! Mom! Wake up!" I slowly opened my eyes to see Ben standing next to the bed looking down on me, wearing nothing but his swimming trunks and goggles. I laughed out loud. He looked so unbelievably cute. I then picked up my watch from the bedside table. It was only eight o'clock and already the sun was streaming through the bedroom window.

"Give me a few minutes to get ready," I said. "And put a t-shirt and shorts on over your trunks, Ben. We need to go for breakfast first."

"Oh, no!" whined Ben.

"Yes, Ben. It's too early to go swimming yet anyway. The water will probably be too cold. It needs the sun on it for a while longer to warm it up."

Less than half an hour later, Ben and I were in the restaurant, helping ourselves to the breakfast buffet. It was fairly quiet, most guests preferring to wander down for breakfast a little later no doubt. But then most guests didn't have Ben with them. Ben piled up his plate with just about everything from the hot buffet; scrambled eggs, beans, sausages, mushrooms……he even added a croissant to the plate. I smiled as I watched him. He was obviously hungrier than he previously let on. After we had chosen a table and Ben had sat down, already beginning to tuck into his hearty breakfast, I filled two glasses with orange juice from the cold drinks machine. After delivering them to the table, I poured myself a coffee.

"Isn't Daddy coming?" asked Ben, his mouth full of sausage.

"Try not to speak with your mouth full," I chided. "I think Daddy was very tired, so it's best to let him sleep. I'm sure he'll get some breakfast when he gets up."

∞

After breakfast, Ben and I made our way to the pool. After dipping his toes in the water, it was some time before Ben was brave enough to get in. Once he was in though, he was reluctant to get back out. "Mom! " Ben called out to me. "Aren't you getting in?"

"Maybe in a little while," I said. I wasn't tempted to leave my sunbed yet as the water still didn't look warm enough to me.

Just then Ben let out a squeal of delight. I turned my head towards the direction he was looking to see Adam walking towards us with a large inflatable shark under his arm.

"Where did you get that from?" I asked.

"The hotel shop," replied Adam. "Here, Ben," he said, throwing it into the water. Ben eagerly swam and splashed his way towards it.

"Thanks Dad!" he called out.

"That was nice of you," I smiled.

"It should keep Ben happy for a while at least."

"Have you had any breakfast?"

"No, I'll get something to eat from the pool bar in a little while," said Adam. "Would you like a drink now?"

"Yes, I'll have a coffee, please," I replied.

I watched Adam head towards the pool bar and wondered if he was already planning to start drinking. As he returned with two mugs of coffee, I decided not to mention last night, unless he did first. There was probably no point in bringing it up again and arguing about it now, although I wondered just how much of last night Adam actually remembered.

After about an hour, Ben managed to persuade Adam to get into the pool with him. I had moved my sunbed into the shade as I was beginning to feel the heat of the sun burning my shoulders. "I could do with cooling off now in the pool," said Adam, his brown skin beginning to glisten with hundreds of tiny beads of sweat.

Ben loved it when Adam played with him, especially as Adam's games were usually much rougher than mine. I watched and smiled as Adam lifted Ben up into the air, then threw him like a giant rag doll back into the water. "Careful!" I called out. But Ben was loving it and just kept coming back for more.

Later that day, after our evening meal, Adam and I patiently sat through the hotel's entertainment programme followed by the kids' disco. Sometimes the entertainment was half-way enjoyable and they certainly seemed to be trying their best. Ben always got up to dance and what he lacked in rhythm and ability, he more than made up for in enthusiasm. He and the other boys he had made friends with over the past couple of days usually ended up seeing how high each of them could pogo or how far each of them could slide along the polished floor. Ben was always a sociable child and full of self-confidence; he was very much like Adam in that respect. Ben always made friends on holiday and Adam couldn't sit close to anybody for very long without striking up a conversation. In those days, everywhere that Adam went, everyone seemed to like him and because of his charm, people would generally overlook any faults he may have had.

∞

The remainder of the holiday went by reasonably smoothly. Adam continued to drink but didn't really overdo it, at least not by his standards. Ben seemed to have a great time, and that's what really mattered most, to me at least. Compared to me, Adam and Ben had such deep tans when we returned to England, you could be forgiven if you assumed we had taken separate holidays. I especially enjoyed waiting for the photos I had taken to be developed. Half of the ones featuring me were discarded. But Adam and Ben on the other hand looked great in every shot. One of those I later framed and had kept on display ever since. It was a photo of Adam and Ben with the inflatable shark, taken on the last day of our holiday. Adam and Ben are both in their shorts and t-shirts, sporting deep golden tans which served to highlight the whiteness of their smiles. They both looked so natural and so happy. And it reminded me of how happy and proud I probably was at that precise moment when I took the picture.

CHAPTER TWENTY-TWO

The days faded into years and the years slipped away. Ben grew up. He did well at school and secured a place at University to study Product design. It was the first time Ben had been away from home for more than a couple of weeks at a time. He was still in his first year and had come home for Christmas. I was surprised at how much I had missed him and how much he seemed to have grown up in such a short span of time. It was Christmas day and Adam was cooking. Most of the time we shared the cooking but Adam usually cooked the Christmas dinner, partly because he was a better cook than me.

"Are you sure you're okay about cooking Christmas dinner this year?" I had asked Adam.

"Yeah, of course, I'll be fine," he had replied.

Adam was in the kitchen checking on the turkey when I suggested Ben and I take Susie out for a walk before I drove over to my dad's to pick him up. Dad usually came to us for Christmas dinner. He had always got on quite well with Adam.

"That's fine," said Adam. "Dinner will be a while yet anyway."

Susie began jumping up excitedly when she saw me holding her lead. "Keep still, or else we won't be taking you out for a walk," I scolded gently, as I attempted to attach her lead to her collar. Susie was Ben's dog really. I had always felt a bit guilty about not having another child. I hated being an only child myself, but then I had deprived Ben of something I could have given him: a younger brother or sister. So I had always tried to compensate by encouraging close friendships with other children and by allowing him to have pets.

We had visited the local dog pound for stray dogs. It was very overcrowded as although they were legally allowed to put any dog down after seven days of admission, as Mary explained to us, they rarely did. Mary was one of the women who worked there. I guessed she was around my age but a lot bigger. She had a ruddy complexion and seemed to be wearing little make-up, if any at all. Her brown hair was scraped back into a pony-tail and she was wearing an oversized polo shirt over a pair of jeans. As she led us to the kennels, we could hear the discordant sound of tens, maybe hundreds of dogs barking. As we walked past the cages containing a collection of different size dogs, some recognisable breeds, others not, some jumping up at the sides of the cages, some cowering in corners, we eventually spotted one dog who seemed just what we were looking for. A medium sized black dog with a short glossy coat, white socks and a flash of white down her chest. Her ears were pricked and her tail was wagging furiously, seemingly in anticipation of being adopted. "Can you bring this one out?" I asked Mary, pointing at the black dog with the white socks.

Mary opened the gate of the cage and slipped a rope collar attached to a lead over the dog's head and led her out to us. Ben stooped down and nearly toppled over as the dog jumped up at him, licking his face. "I love her!" he exclaimed, trying to cuddle her as her whole body now seemed to wag along with her tail.

"We think she's probably about a year old," explained Mary. A Labrador-terrier cross. "

"Where did she come from?" I asked.

"She was found wandering nearby without a collar on, so the Police picked her up and brought her here. Nobody's turned up to claim her."

"Well she certainly seems very friendly," I said, smiling. "Do you want her, Ben?"

"Yes please!" said Ben excitedly. Ben was eleven years old and we had finally agreed he could have a dog, believing he was now old enough to take some responsibility for taking care of one.

Susie was now around nine years old and what with Ben away at university, I had taken over full responsibility for taking care of her.

It was a lovely December day. The air was cool and crisp, but the sky was blue and the sun was shining. "I've met someone," said Ben. "Someone really nice."

I looked at Ben who was walking beside me, holding Susie's lead. She always pulled less when Ben was walking her. "Really?" I beamed. "What's her name?"

"Anita."

"Well, tell me all about her."

"She's the same age as me," began Ben. "She's got long dark hair. She's really pretty but not big headed about it, if you know what I mean?"

"What's she studying?" I asked.

"Social Sciences."

"Well when are we going to meet her?" I asked.

"I don't know. Perhaps I'll bring her here to meet you next time I'm home for the holidays?"

"That'll be great."

"How's Dad?" asked Ben, changing the subject.

"Well he hasn't been so well I'm afraid."

Ben was silent for a moment. "Is it the drink?"

"No, no," I said. "Well I don't think that helped, but he's stopped drinking now, so….."

"Has he?"

"Yes."

"Are you sure about that?" asked Ben. He sounded dubious.

"Yeah, I'm sure. " But then I got the feeling Ben didn't believe me.

"And how are you, Mum?" asked Ben.

"I'm okay," I said. "I'm very busy at work. I just get very tired these days. But that's getting old for you."

"You're not old!" laughed Ben.

"Well sometimes I only feel about twenty-one……in here I mean," I said, tapping my head with my fingers. "In fact, I wonder where all the years have gone. But then other times, I feel about a hundred and one!"

"Well you only look about twenty-one to me," said Ben.

"Ah, Ben, you always know the right things to say," I said, smiling, linking my arm in his.

As I opened the front door, we were met by the slightly reminiscent smell of turkey cooking in the oven. "Hold on, Susie!" I said, as she began trotting towards the kitchen. "Wipe your feet." Susie stopped and obediently lifted each paw in turn, allowing me to dry her paws with the spare towel I kept by the door in the hallway.

Ben dutifully took off his shoes before making his way into the sitting room. "Mom!" he called out as I hung up my coat.

"What is it?" I asked, as I headed towards the sitting room.

Adam was fast asleep on the settee, snoring. I went over to Adam and shook him. "What?" he groaned, without opening his eyes.

"Adam! Adam!" I shouted in his ear. I shook him again. This time he opened his eyes which were glazed and bloodshot. He then attempted to stand up. Ben helped him up. Adam then staggered into the hallway and began to climb the stairs. "Where are you going?" I asked.

"To bed," was his reply.

I didn't bother arguing. He was obviously drunk. Maybe it would be better, I thought, if I just let him sleep it off. I went back into the sitting room. Ben was sat down now on the edge of the settee with Susie sat beside him on the floor, stroking her behind her ears. He looked up at me as I entered the room. I didn't know what to say. I felt so embarrassed. "I don't know what to do about the dinner," I said finally. "I've got to leave shortly to pick Granddad up."

"You go and pick Granddad up," said Ben. "I'll look after the dinner." Ben was almost as good a cook as Adam, or rather as Adam used to be.

"Are you sure you don't mind? I feel awful. We were supposed to be cooking dinner for *you*."

"Don't feel bad," reassured Ben. "It's not your fault."

I gave Ben an awkward smile. Ben, my little boy, was a man now. I could no longer shield him from those images I didn't want him to see, or those things I didn't want him to know. "Okay, I'll get going then."

As I opened the driver's door of my car which was on the drive, Ben who was standing in the doorway of the house, holding Susie by her collar, said, "do you just want me to let Dad sleep?"

"Yes, for now," I said.

As I was driving over to Dad's, I could feel the anger and frustration building up inside me. Then a gentle trickle of tears ran down my cheeks. I pulled into a layby just five minutes away from Dad's. I needed to touch up my make-up. I didn't want Dad to know I'd been crying.

When I pulled up outside Dad's, he was at the door before I managed to switch off the engine. I was a little late. He'd probably been waiting anxiously at the window, but he would never admit to that. "Sorry I'm late," I said, as Dad got into the car next to me.

"That's okay," he said, as he belted up. I noticed he had several envelopes in his hands, no doubt containing money for Adam, Ben and myself. He never knew what to get us, so always gave us money, which Ben especially appreciated. "Is Adam cooking dinner?"

I hesitated. "Yeah, with some help from Ben." I wondered whether I should mention the fact that Adam may not actually be having dinner with us now. If I didn't say anything, Dad would probably wonder why I hadn't. Having said that, by the time I arrived back home with Dad, Adam may have got up again. In a way, I hoped he hadn't. I hoped he would remain upstairs in bed until after I had left with Dad to drive him back home. "Adam hasn't been feeling very well," I began, "so I'm afraid he may not be joining us for dinner."

"Oh, dear," said Dad, "sorry to hear that." Dad had always liked Adam and generally got on well with him. I wondered if he would have had the same regard for him if he had known him as well as he thought he did.

"He went upstairs for a lie down just before I left, so hopefully he'll be feeling better later."

∞

"My compliments to the chef," said Dad, as he tucked into the roast dinner Ben had taken over cooking half way through.

"Yeah this is really nice, Ben," I said. However I couldn't enjoy it as much as I would have liked. Adam should have been sat at the table with us. Instead he was conspicuous by his absence.

"Well it was a joint effort really," said Ben, giving me a knowing glance.

"Yeah it's a shame Adam's not feeling well," said Dad. I wondered if Dad really believed that story or whether he secretly realised the truth.

Ben and Dad were now relaxing in the sitting room while I did the washing up. "I'll bring some coffee through when I've finished," I said.

"That'll be lovely, Fay," said Dad.

I was just scrubbing out the saucepans when I thought I caught site of something in the corner of my eye. I turned my head and sure enough someone was stood in the door-way. It was Adam. "My God!" I exclaimed. "You nearly gave me a heart attack! Do you *have* to creep around like that?"

"I'm not creeping around," said Adam. He was dressed but his hair was sticking out in all directions, his eyes still puffy with sleep. "What time are you going to pick your Dad up?"

"I already have," I said. "He's in the sitting room with Ben."

"Oh. Well what about dinner?"

"We've had ours," I said. "I've plated yours up for you if you want it. It's in the microwave. It just needs heating up."

"Why did you have dinner without me?"

"Because you weren't here. You were in bed remember?" I said. "Pissed."

"I wasn't pissed," said Adam. "I was just tired."

I didn't want to argue about it now. At least not while Dad and Ben were in the house. "I told Dad you weren't feeling very well, although Ben knows differently."

"What do you mean?"

"He knows you were pissed."

"I told you I wasn't pissed, and I resent the accusation." Adam's tone was becoming increasingly vexed.

"Ok, can we just draw a line under it, Adam, and salvage something of the rest of the day?"

"That's fine by me," said Adam, curtly. "I'll go and say hello to your Dad."

Fortunately the rest of the day went by without incident, although I constantly felt on edge, as I watched Adam pour himself one drink after another. Eventually he just crashed out on the settee.

CHAPTER TWENTY-THREE

By the time Ben and Anita had both finished University, they were moving in together, and within a couple of years Anita was pregnant. Ben had a good job and could afford to support them while Anita took time off to have a child. It wasn't until they discovered she was having twins that Anita decided to give up work altogether for a while, or at least until they started school.

Emily and Jessica were born at the start of the Summer. They were non-identical twins but neither one was more beautiful than the other. We were a little worried that Ben and Anita had started a family too soon, but they both had a very mature yet laid back attitude and proved to be wonderful parents. I was so proud of Ben. I wondered if I told him that enough.

"Ben rang earlier," I told Adam on Wednesday. "They're having a birthday party for Jessica and Emily on Saturday and would like us to come."

"What time?"

"Around three. They're hiring a bouncy castle."

"Bouncy castles aren't really my thing." I assumed Adam was joking, so I just ignored this last remark.

"So will you be coming with me?"

"Yeah, of course," said Adam. "I haven't seen them for a while. It would be nice to spend some time with them." Adam hadn't seen them for a while because the last couple of times I had visited, I had gone alone.

∞

It was Saturday. I went into town in the morning to finish buying presents for the twins, but before I left, I reminded Adam about the party. "We need to leave about 2.30," I said.

"Yeah, no problem."

At 12.30 Adam was putting on his fleece jacket and his shoes. "Where are you going?" I asked.

"Just for a quick drink at the Black Swan," he replied.

"Do you *have* to? You can have a drink when we get to Ben's."

"We've got plenty of time." Adam picked up his wallet and keys. "I won't be long. Will you pick me up on the way?"

"Don't you want to see what I've got for the girls before I wrap them up?"

"I'm sure whatever you've got them will be great," said Adam. "Are you going to pick me up or not?"

"Yeah, okay," I said, begrudgingly. "Make sure you're outside at 2.30 then. I don't want to have to go inside."

I pulled up outside the Black Swan at 2.30 exactly. Adam wasn't stood outside as he promised. I sighed heavily and muttered to myself, "typical!"

I waited about five minutes, although it seemed much longer. I switched off the engine, got out of the car and climbed the couple of old stone steps into the pub.

Adam was sitting at the bar with almost a full pint in his hand, chatting and laughing without a care in the world. I stood there for a second or two before he even noticed me. "Oh hi, Fay!" he said, cheerily. "Do you want a drink?"

"No," I said, curtly. "We're supposed to be going to Ben's, remember?"

"You've got time for a drink, surely?" said Adam, slurring his words.

"How many have you had?"

"I don't know. How many have I had?" Adam leaned towards one of his drinking buddies on the stool next to him, almost knocking him off his perch.

I could feel a lump in my throat. I swallowed hard and lowered my voice, in a vain attempt to avoid being overheard. "Why do you always have to do this?"

"Do what?" asked Adam, almost innocently.

I didn't want to argue in front of other people. I felt like screaming and shouting at him, but instead I remained restrained. "Tell you what," I began, "why don't you stay here and finish your drink? I'll go over to the party and then see you later when I get back."

I often wished Ben lived nearer to us, but today I was glad of the distance. At least it gave me time to calm down and work out what I was going to tell everyone when I turned up without Adam. I don't know why I just didn't tell them the truth. That Adam wasn't coming because he'd rather get pissed up in the pub than see his Granddaughters on their birthday. Was it embarrassment on my part? Or was it because I didn't want to hurt anyone else's feelings? Or was it simply because I didn't want anyone thinking badly of Adam? I wasn't sure.

It was a lovely day for it. It was one of those rare early summer days when the sun was still shining right up until the evening. One of those days when you forget what a grey sky looks like, when you forget what it feels like to be cold and wet. I had told everyone that Adam hadn't been feeling well. It was probably a bug which he didn't want to pass on to the girls. I wondered if they believed me as I had used this excuse before, probably more times than I cared to remember.

Jessica and Emily loved their presents. Ben and Anita gently chided me for spoiling them yet again. I told the girls that Granddad sent his love and although the presents were from both of us, Ben and Anita knew it was always me who remembered their birthdays, then chose and bought their presents.

I was seated next to Anita in a deckchair on the lawn. I had grown to love Anita, almost like the daughter I had never had. We watched Jessica and Emily on the large inflatable castle, energetically bouncing around with their little friends from school and from down the street, all yelping with excitement. "They seem to be really enjoying themselves," I smiled.

"Yes, I think the bouncy castle was a great idea," said Anita. "And we've been so lucky with the weather."

I nodded.

"There's some burgers ready, if anyone would like one?" Ben called out. As per usual, he had taken charge of the barbeque. Several of the children immediately leapt off the bouncy castle to be first in line for a burger. "Mum, would you like a burger?"

"Give the children theirs first," I replied. "I'll have mine in a minute, thanks."

"Would you like another drink?" asked Anita.

"You know, I'd love a cup of tea, if you don't mind?"

"Yeah of course," replied Anita0, getting up.

"I'll make it if you like?" I offered.

“No, no, you stay there,” said Anita, “I’ll get it. Just relax.” I smiled. It was rather nice to be waited on. It didn’t happen very often.

I stayed until the sun began to make its slow descent towards the horizon. Even then I felt reluctant to leave but did not want to outstay my welcome. In fact I realised that I was feeling quite apprehensive about returning home. I used to look forward to seeing Adam and would miss him dreadfully when we were apart. Now I could barely remember what that felt like.

CHAPTER TWENTY-FOUR

We had been invited out for a meal by Alison and Brian. They were in town for a short while and had decided to catch up with old friends. We hadn't seen them for years. Julia and Tony had also been invited whom we had seen more recently, but it was still good to see them again. We arranged to all meet in the Italian restaurant where a table had been booked for seven-thirty.

I had begged Adam not to have a drink before we went out, to at least wait until we got to the restaurant, but I suspected he had because he seemed immediately at ease in the company of our friends. I wondered however what was going through their minds when they saw Adam. Even though we hadn't seen Brian for so long, he looked much the same despite putting on a little bit of weight. Alison now had her hair cut sensibly short whereas it used to be long. I didn't think that I had changed that much but Adam undoubtedly had. He had put on a lot of weight, his face was bloated and the whites of his eyes were always red. His hair was now almost completely grey. He had aged beyond his years. I felt that Brian was probably making every effort not to show his true feelings, but the look in his eyes betrayed the shock and concern he felt on seeing the change in Adam. Nevertheless, the evening began well. As we chatted with Alison and Brian, the years that had separated us melted away. However as the evening wore on, I became more and more anxious the more Adam drank. We had just finished our desserts when Adam attracted the attention of one of the waiters who immediately came over to our table. "Could I order another bottle of red, please?" he asked.

"A bottle? Are you sure you want a bottle?" I questioned him, as quietly as I could but loud enough for him to hear.

"Yeah, a bottle, that's what I said. Is there a problem?" Adam challenged, and his voice was rather too loud. "Does anyone else want a drink?"

"No, I'm fine," they all seemed to say in unison.

"Can I have a coffee please?" I asked, trying to make my voice sound as normal as possible. "A latte."

"Oh, I think I'll have a coffee too!" exclaimed Alison, as though the thought had not occurred to her before I suggested it myself. "A cappuccino, please. Anyone else want coffee?" The rest of our party shook their heads.

The waiter nodded and walked away.

Adam then attempted to stand up. "Where are you going?" I asked.

"The toilet," stated Adam. "Is that okay with you?" His tone was sarcastic.

"Of course," I replied. "I was just wondering".

I watched Adam stand up and try to extricate himself from his chair. Then as he began to walk away from the table, his legs seemed to run away with him as he landed virtually head first into a neighbouring table, knocking several glasses over. The woman at the table stood up and jumped back suddenly as the wine from the upturned glasses ran in rivulets towards the edges of the table. "I'm so sorry," Adam slurred but the man and woman at the table just threw him icy glares. Once Adam managed to stand up straight again, he made his way towards the toilets without a glance over his shoulder at us. I wondered if he was going to offer to buy the couple some more drinks, but it didn't look like he was going to. The air suddenly felt very heavy as we all sat in silence at the table. I avoided everyone's gaze although I knew what they were all thinking. Eventually Julia broke the silence. "Has anyone got any holidays booked this year?" she asked randomly, her voice sounding higher than usual. At that point the waiter delivered the bottle of red wine Adam had ordered. He removed the cork and poured a little into my glass to try. I nodded and he continued to fill the glass. I didn't want any wine so I don't know why I just didn't say that, but once he had started to pour the wine, it seemed easier to just say nothing. He then went to pour some wine into Alison's glass but she placed her hand over it, indicating she didn't want any.

"You can just leave the bottle here," I suggested.

When Adam arrived back at the table the waiter was also delivering our coffees. I moved the glass of wine towards Adam. He looked at me perplexed so I explained that the waiter thought I was also drinking wine. I resisted the temptation of saying *most normal people would share a bottle of wine rather than drink it all themselves.* I didn't want to provoke an argument. Adam drank the glass of wine virtually in one gulp. I gingerly sipped my coffee as it was still very hot. Adam immediately poured himself another glass and drank that one as quickly as the first. Alison hadn't even tried her coffee yet. I wished she would hurry up. I continued to sip mine even though it was really too hot, burning the roof of my mouth as I did so. I think I was subconsciously hoping that this would encourage Alison to drink hers. I wanted someone to say they needed to leave now. Was I the only one who was feeling so uncomfortable? Adam wasn't likely to want to leave. I wanted more than anything for this evening to be over before anything else embarrassing happened, but it would seem oddly conspicuous for me to leave without Adam. Unless I said I was suddenly feeling unwell. Yes, I could say that. "I'm really sorry everyone, but I'm afraid I'll have to go," I announced.

"Go?" they all seemed to echo in unison.

"Yeah I think I'm getting one of my bad headaches," I explained, as convincingly as I could.

"Oh dear," said Alison, with genuine concern in her voice. "I hope you feel better soon."

Immediately I felt a little guilty, as only I knew that her concern was really quite unwarranted, and more importantly, undeserved. "Yeah, I'll be fine, thank you," I replied. "I just need to get some sleep."

"Well, it's been lovely to see you," said Alison, smiling.

"It's been lovely seeing you too. All of you." I smiled warmly at everyone seated at the table. Except for Adam. "Will you be coming with me, Adam, or are you staying here?"

"Do you mind if I stay?" Adam asked. "I haven't seen Brian for so long."

"No, that's fine. I'll just ring for a taxi."

After kissing all our friends good-bye, I left and took the taxi home. Once I arrived, I went into the kitchen and poured myself a glass of water which I carried upstairs and placed on the table next to my side of the bed. I then went through my usual bedtime ritual of cleaning my teeth and removing my make-up, before changing into my night clothes. I read for a few minutes once I was in bed but I was having difficulty concentrating. Then suddenly I realised just how tired I was, so I switched off the bedside lamp. I think I fell asleep soon after my head hit the pillow.

I woke with a start. Someone was knocking on the front door and ringing the bell. I jumped out of bed and after putting on my dressing gown, padded downstairs. When I opened the door, I was faced with the sight of Adam, his head hanging down so that it was almost touching his chest, with his arms around Brian and Tony's shoulders who were trying to support his weight. For what was probably only a split second, but seemed so much longer, I stood unable to move, my mouth agape, trying to mentally register the unexpected sight before my eyes. "He sort of collapsed," explained Brian. "We didn't really know what to do. We thought about taking him to the hospital but Adam refused to go. I think he's just had a bit too much to drink."

"That's okay," I said, as calmly as possible, whilst inwardly seething.

"Do you want us to try to get him upstairs?"

I wondered how they would manage to do that, so said "no, don't worry, just bring him through to the sitting room if you can and he can sleep it off on the settee." I didn't really want Adam in bed with me anyway.

∞

The next day, the tension in the air was almost palpable. At first neither of us mentioned the evening before. Adam tried to behave as though nothing had happened. But my silence said it all. He knew I was angry. Eventually, it was Adam who relented and brought up the subject first. He had followed me into the kitchen where I proceeded to make myself a cup of tea, without asking him if he wanted one too. "Look I know you're angry, and I'm really sorry, but how long are you going to keep up this silent treatment?"

I let out a deep sigh. Then without looking up, I said, "I don't think I can do this anymore."

For a moment Adam was speechless. "What are you saying? Do you want to split up?"

"Maybe."

"Surely you don't want to throw our marriage away just because I drank a bit too much last night?"

"It's not just because of last night though. It's because of all the other nights and days you've ruined by drinking too much. I'm afraid I'm going to end up hating you, and I don't want that." I was stood facing Adam now.

"What do you want me to do?"

"You should already know that without me having to tell you. I've told you enough times before."

"To stop drinking. That's what you want, isn't it?"

"Ideally, yes."

"Okay, I'll do it," said Adam, emphatically.

"Just like that?"

"Yes. Just like that."

CHAPTER TWENTY-FIVE

Adam was true to his word because he did stop drinking then. But he didn't look well. He often broke out in cold sweats. He was shaking and began to vomit. Neither of us realised at the time that what he was experiencing was in fact withdrawal. In fact Adam put his symptoms down to flu and the last thing he felt like doing was having another drink.

After a couple of days however, Adam was now starting to feel a lot better however and had even felt like eating something. It was evening and I had cooked us a nice meal: spaghetti Bolognese. As I spooned the gently bubbling sauce onto a bed of spaghetti, I recalled the first time I had ever tasted spaghetti Bolognese. It was the first meal Adam had ever cooked for me, all those years ago.....

We were now sat beside one another on the settee and had just finished watching a film. "I think I'll go up now," I said. I then leant forward to give him a quick kiss goodnight on the cheek, but stopped and drew back, because suddenly something strange was happening. Adam's face appeared to be twitching, as though he had developed some sort of weird tic. Sheer panic was reflected in his eyes. "What's wrong?"

Adam raised his hand up to his head as though he was trying to work out what was happening to him. Then suddenly his head jerked violently to the side and his face contorted into a grotesque grimace. He let out a horrific cry. Then his body and face relaxed again as he began to convulse, his eyes still open but vacant now like the eyes of the dead. As the convulsion came to an end, his breathing became laboured. Then just when I thought it was all over, his whole body became rigid once again as he let out another blood curdling cry before convulsing yet again. By now he had slid down so that he was half sitting and half lying on the settee. I was so shocked, it took me until then to realise what was happening and that I needed to call for help. I was now kneeling on the floor in front of Adam as I dialled 999 on my mobile phone.

"Emergency. Which service do you require?" came the voice at the other end of the phone.

"Ambulance, please."

Then a different voice. "Are you the patient?"

"No, it's my husband." I could hear my voice shaking now.

"Are you with him?"

"Yes."

"Can you give me your address and the number you are calling from."

I reeled off the address and my mobile phone number.

"What's your husband's name?"

"Adam. Adam Reynolds," I replied.

"How old is he?"

"He's 54."

"Is he conscious?"

"I don't think so. His eyes are open, but I don't think so. I think he might be having a fit." I could feel my whole body shaking now.

"Is he lying down?"

"Yeah, he's sort of slumped on the settee."

"Okay, don't try to move him. Just let him finish fitting and then if you can, put him into the recovery position." I knew that would be impossible, unless I dragged him off the settee on to the floor first.

"Is an ambulance coming?" I said, impatiently. In retrospect, that seemed like a silly question.

"Yes, don't worry an ambulance is on its way. Please stay on the line."

"Okay."

"Is he still breathing?"

"Yes, but he's making a horrible sound.....can you hear him?"

"Yes, that's okay, that's normal," came the woman's voice. She sounded so calm. "The ambulance should be outside now. Can you let them in?"

I jumped up from the floor and went to the door. Two paramedics were already making their way up the garden path, one carrying a huge backpack, like something out of *Ghostbusters*.

"Thank you, they're here," I said.

"Okay, you can hang up now."

I showed the Paramedics into the front room where Adam was still on the settee but was now sitting upright. "Hello.....is it Adam?"

Adam just stared at the Paramedic, bewildered. "Yes, it's Adam," I answered for him. The Paramedic unzipped the backpack and began to take out a variety of instruments. With well-practised expertise, leads were attached to Adam's chest, arms and legs; and a pulse oximeter was attached to his index finger. A cuff was wrapped around Adam's arm which one Paramedic then proceeded to inflate. I held Adam's other hand in an attempt to keep him calm and still.

"Can you tell me your date of birth, Adam?"

Again I answered for him. "It's the 15th of September, 1956."

"His oxygen saturation level's a little low," said the other Paramedic. "Otherwise, everything's fine." He removed all the leads and the cuff from his arm. "I think we'll take him in anyway, just to be on the safe side."

"Do you think they'll keep him in?" I asked.

"They might do."

"I'll put a few things in a bag for him then," I said.

"If you can put any medication he's on in as well, that'll be very helpful."

I quickly climbed the stairs and went into our bedroom. I opened the cupboard above the built in wardrobe. I was sure there was a small holdall in there. Sure enough there was. I dragged it out and dropped it on the bed. I then opened Adam's chest of drawers and took out some clean socks and underwear, plus a t-shirt and jogging bottoms. He had no pyjamas so those would have to do. I then went into the bathroom and collected together a handful of his toiletries and a razor. I went back down stairs into the kitchen where he kept his tablets and put those in the bag as well. I then picked up his shoes from the hallway before returning to the front room. Adam was still sat on the settee but the expression on his face was now less confused. I slipped off his slippers, putting them into the holdall, and then put his shoes on for him. Putting someone else's shoes on for them is surprisingly difficult. "Push your foot down," I instructed as I tried to pull the back of the shoe over his heel.

Eventually I managed to get his shoes on and tie them up. The Paramedics then helped Adam stand. "Let's see if you can walk," one of them said. "That's it, take your time."

With their help, Adam managed to walk out of the house and into the ambulance. "I'll follow in my car, shall I?" I said.

"Yes, that'll be great if you could. We'll be taking him to St Anne's."

I followed the ambulance all the way to the hospital, some fourteen miles away. A couple of times I thought I'd lost them, but I knew where I was going anyway. It wasn't the first time I had been to St Anne's.

By the time I arrived at the hospital, they had already taken Adam inside. I approached the desk in the Accident & Emergency department. "My husband's just been brought in here," I explained.

"What's his name, please?" asked the woman at the desk.

"It's Adam Reynolds."

"I'll just check for you," she said, leaving the desk.

A couple of minutes later she returned. "He's in cubicle 3," she said. "You can go on through if you like."

"Thanks."

I wandered around for a few seconds, trying to work out which was cubicle 3. The walls of the cubicles were merely curtains, so you could hear everything that was going on or being said behind them. Then I spied Adam through a gap in one of the curtains, lying on his back on a trolley, half-sitting up. "Oh, hi Fay!" he said, without a care in the world, as I walked over to him. "I'm glad you're here." It seemed Adam had fully recovered and was back to his usual self. In fact he seemed unusually cheerful, considering the circumstances. I was the one who was really shook up. "I'm just waiting to see the doctor."

"Do you remember what happened?" I asked.

"Apparently I had a seizure," said Adam.

"Yeah you did. In fact you had two, one after the other. It scared me half to death."

Just then, a dark featured doctor appeared. "How are you, Mr Reynolds?" he asked.

"I'm okay I think, considering. A bit worried though. Apparently I had two seizures."

"Yes that's right, you did. Have you ever had any before?"

"No, not that I'm aware of," said Adam.

"Apparently you are a heavy drinker."

"Yes, I must admit I am. But I want to stop. I've cut down a lot over the past few days."

"Were you doing this under any medical supervision or were you just doing it by yourself?" asked the doctor.

"Just by myself."

"That's obviously why you had the fits. Do you realise how dangerous that is?" the doctor admonished.

"No, I didn't," said Adam, rather sheepishly.

"What we can do for you is to keep you in so that we can help you detox safely with the right medication, so that you don't have any more seizures. That's if you want to stop drinking, of course."

"Yes I do," said Adam.

"Ok, as soon as we find you a bed, we'll admit you. Meanwhile, we'll take you for a scan just to make sure the fits haven't caused a bleed."

"Are you taking him for a scan now?" I asked.

"Yes, in a couple of minutes or so."

"I'll say good bye now then," I said. "I need to get back if I'm going to get up for work tomorrow."

"Okay," said Adam, leaning forward with the expectation of a kiss. I planted a quick kiss on his lips before making my way back out to my car.

CHAPTER TWENTY-SIX

I felt exhausted by the time I got to bed that night and still felt exhausted the following morning for I had had very little sleep. But I still got up for work as usual. I made myself a cup of tea but couldn't face breakfast. Then as I followed the long line of traffic along the familiar route to work, I turned the events of the previous evening over and over in my mind.

I wondered whether Adam had actually been drinking more than he had led me to believe. I also wondered why he needed to drink so much. He had always liked a drink, but at what point had it become the number one priority in his life? What was it about our life together that was so bad and so painful that Adam needed to escape from it so desperately, needed to expunge it from his consciousness? Was it my fault? Had I driven him to it? I cast my mind back over the years to try to make sense of it all. I recalled one event that I knew had caused Adam so much pain at the time and had haunted us both ever since.....

It was a long time ago, before Ben was born. Even before we were married. We were at a New Year's Eve party at a friend of a friend's house. We had arrived early and we stayed until after one in the morning. The trouble is when you drink at a house party, no one really monitors how much you are really drinking, especially not you. I wasn't used to drinking a lot, which was all the more reason why I shouldn't have had that fifth rum and coke, or the sixth, or the seventh. After that I lost count. There was someone else at the party I had not met before. His name was Colin. He was good looking, but not as good looking as Adam. So I don't really know why I did what I did. In fact I still don't know why. I blamed the alcohol but a part of me still knew what I was doing. For some reason I didn't seem to care. I knew Adam would probably find out. I wonder if I was testing him, testing our relationship, or subconsciously sabotaging it, destroying what we had before he had a chance to. Because it all seemed too good to be true. Adam seemed too good to be true.

I don't know whose bedroom it was but the bed we were lying on was covered with other people's coats. I only have a very bleary memory of what we did but I know we were both half undressed when Adam opened the door. Someone had seen us sneaking into the bedroom and felt they needed to tell Adam. Adam didn't even turn the light on. He just left the room, the door still wide open. Colin jumped off of me and quickly tucked in his shirt and did up his trousers. A few seconds later I began to follow Colin out of the room, but just as I reached the open doorway, Colin fell backwards, almost knocking me over and landing flat on his back on the floor. At first I wasn't sure what had happened. Then I saw two of Adam's friends on either side of him, holding him back. Adam was very angry and was shouting "you fucking bastard!" I had not seen Adam as angry as that before. In fact I don't think I had even seen Adam really angry at all until that night. I realised then that Adam had hit Colin. Eventually they let Adam go and he left the party. Against my better judgement I followed him.

When I got outside it was raining hard. Adam was already half-way up the street. I ran after him, shouting his name, but he kept on going without breaking his stride. Eventually I reached him, grabbing the back of his leather jacket. Adam stopped abruptly and swung round. I didn't feel the punches, possibly because the vast amount of alcohol I had drunk had numbed my senses. One minute I was standing upright, the next minute I was on my hands and knees on the wet ground. I looked up to see Adam disappearing around the corner, his image blurred by my tears and the unforgiving rain that continued to fall.

I don't know how long I was on the ground for, but eventually I managed to drag myself up and somehow make my way home. I then realised I'd forgotten my handbag with my key inside. I'd left it at the party. So I rang the bell. I heard it ring inside but Adam never came to the door. I knocked as loudly as I could but still he did not let me in. I then wondered if he had actually come home at all as the house seemed to be in total darkness. I started to panic. How was I going to get in? There was no way I was going back to the party, and I could not contact anyone. I was too embarrassed, too ashamed. Suddenly I remembered the spare key under the flower pot by the door. I prayed that it was still there. I breathed a sigh of relief when I found it. A few seconds later I was in the hallway. I turned on the light and then caught sight of my face in the mirror on the wall. I almost didn't recognise myself. My wet hair was flat against my head, my eyes puffed up from the tears I had wept, and my split lip was swollen and still bleeding. That made me start crying all over again. What had I done? I had ruined everything.

I climbed the stairs, washed my face in the bathroom and then went into the bedroom. Adam was already in bed. I didn't turn on the light but left the door open so I could get undressed by the light from the landing. I slid into bed next to Adam although I half-expected him to tell me to "fuck off!" Instead, rather surprisingly, he draped an arm around me. He didn't speak so I wondered whether he was actually awake. I moved closer to him so that I could feel his breath on the back of my neck. Despite what Adam had done, I wanted nothing more than his arm around me now.

When I awoke it was light and Adam was already up. I got out of bed and put on my dressing gown. I went down stairs to find Adam in the sitting room reading the newspaper. He glanced at me but then looked back at the paper when he spoke. "I'm sorry for what I did to you. But you have no idea how much you hurt me."

"I'm sorry," I said. "Do you want me to leave?"

"No," Adam replied. "But if you'd rather be with Colin or some other bloke, I think it's best that you do."

"I don't want to be with anyone else," I said. "I don't know why I did it. I was far too drunk. I promise it will never happen again."

Adam was silent for a moment. "Okay, let's just draw a line under it, shall we?" His tone was still cold and curt.

Things were never really quite the same after that. We both tried to forget it but the love we had felt for one another was now tarnished. I forgave Adam for hitting me. I told myself that we were even, although for a long time I felt just a little bit scared of him. I knew what Adam was capable of now.

∞

I felt a sudden jolt that propelled me back to reality. I hadn't realised that the car in front of me had stopped so I had driven into the back of it. Fortunately I had only been travelling around twenty miles an hour, probably less, so if I was lucky, I may not have done any damage. The person who was driving the car in front got out.

"Oh no!" I said out loud. "Shit! Shit!"

The person who had got out of the car was a young woman who looked around eight or nine months pregnant. I unfastened my seat belt and got out of my car. "I'm really sorry," I said, with as much sincerity in my voice as I could muster. "I didn't realise you had stopped." The woman said nothing but just glared at me. She then began trying to inspect the back of her car, although it was difficult for her to ascertain how much damage I had done, considering the front of my car was still touching the back of hers.

"I will have to ring the police," the woman said eventually.

"Okay, okay," I said. "I better give you my insurance details." I got back inside my car to search for a pen and some paper. I found an old envelope in my handbag but couldn't find a pen. "Do you have a pen I can borrow?" I asked the woman.

"Yes I think so," she said, returning to her car. I couldn't remember what information I was supposed to give, so I wrote down my name and telephone number, my registration number and my insurance company's details. She seemed satisfied with this. She was already on her phone to the police.

When she hung up, I asked, "do you think we should move our cars over to the side of the road?" I was conscious of the fact that we were half-blocking the road.

"No," she replied, abruptly.

"Oh, okay." I replied. "I just need to ring my boss." I returned again to my car.

I actually rang one of my work colleagues, explaining what had just happened and what had happened the previous evening. "I'll be in a bit late, I'm afraid," I said.

"Don't worry," said Lorna, reassuringly. "I'll let Kath know." Kath was my boss.

By the time I arrived at work I was almost an hour late. I had only done some minor damage to the pregnant woman's car, although I was more concerned about the fact that I may have caused her to go into premature labour. The police who had arrived at the scene were surprisingly understanding. The fact that I was apologising profusely no doubt helped. They recommended the pregnant woman get herself checked out at the hospital but allowed me to go on my way, once they were satisfied that we had exchanged insurance details. They even asked me if I was okay.

My boss was surprisingly understanding as well. When I related the events of the previous night, she smiled knowingly, stating, "my mother was an alcoholic too, so I realise how difficult it can be."

I was slightly taken aback. I had never really considered Adam to be an alcoholic before. A heavy drinker, yes, but not necessarily an alcoholic. But then the more I thought about it, the more I realised, that was precisely what he was.

CHAPTER TWENTY-SEVEN

After work I called in to see Adam at the hospital before going home. He seemed a little edgy but pleased to see me. "Did you ring Tom to let him know I wouldn't be in?" Adam asked me. Tom was Adam's line manager.

"Yeah, I explained what had happened and he seemed genuinely concerned," I said. I had left out the fact that Adam had suffered a seizure because he had previously been drinking so heavily. "I've brought your wallet. In case you need to buy a paper or something." I fished in my handbag for Adam's wallet and handed it to him.

"Have you got my keys as well?" Adam asked.

"No."

"I'd like you to bring my keys in tomorrow."

"Why?" I gave Adam a quizzical look. "You don't need them."

"I just want them, that's all. Just bring them, will you?" Adam was distinctly tetchy.

"Okay, okay," I acquiesced.

By the time I got home, I was so tired I went to bed without any tea. However I slept well that night, relieved that Adam was finally getting and accepting the help he needed.

I called at the hospital straight after work again. As I walked on to the ward, I noticed that Adam's bed had been stripped bare and he was nowhere to be seen. I turned to one of the nurses who was doing her rounds. "Excuse me, could you tell me where Adam Reynolds is, please? Has he been moved to another ward?"

For a moment her face wore a blank expression. "He's been discharged, I think."

"What?"

"I'll just check with the nurse in charge," she said, as she headed towards the nurses' station. I followed her.

"Yes, Mr Reynolds was discharged about an hour ago," stated the nurse in charge.

"But why?" I asked, in disbelief. "We were told he needed to stay in hospital for at least five days to complete his detox treatment."

"I know, but he was most insistent on leaving," explained the nurse, adding; "it was against medical advice."

"And you let him leave?"

"I felt he had the mental capacity to make that decision," she explained.

"Why didn't you call me?"

I think I might have detected a flash of panic in her eyes. "I don't think we have your telephone number."

"Of course you do. I'm the next of kin."

At that point, I strode off the ward, muttering and cursing under my breath, but knowing full well at the same time that the nurses or the hospital probably weren't to blame.

I drove home, assuming that's where Adam had headed. He had enough money on him for bus fare or a taxi, but not his keys to get in. Then I remembered the spare key we usually kept under the flower pot.

By the time I arrived home it was dark, and the house was in darkness too. I switched the light on in the hallway. "Adam!" I called out, but was merely met with silence. I began searching the house although I was pretty sure he wasn't there. He was nowhere to be found. I let Susie out into the garden and fed her. I then made myself a cup of tea. I sat down on the sofa, sipping my tea, wondering what to do next.

I was a little startled by the ring tone of my phone which was still in my handbag. I fished it out and answered it, not knowing who it was as the screen displayed *unknown number*. "Hello?"

"Is that Mrs Reynolds?"

"Yes?"

"This is the Accident and Emergency Department at Princes Hospital. Your husband has just been brought in by a member of the public. He's had a fall and seems very confused."

"Has he injured himself?"

"We think it's just superficial," the anonymous voice replied, "but are you able to come to the hospital now?"

"Yes, I'm on my way." I realised that my voice was now a little shaky. "It may take me about half an hour to get there though."

"That's fine."

∞

When I arrived at the hospital Adam was with the doctor in one of the cubicles. I could hear Adam's raised voice before I could see him. He was sat on a trolley, attempting to lower himself to the floor, and seemed very agitated. "You can't keep me here!"

"I just want one of my colleagues to have a look at you," said the doctor. His tone was firm yet reassuring, but I could see he was having difficulty calming Adam down.

"Oh, thank God you're here," said Adam as I appeared through a gap in the curtains.

I noticed that Adam had scuffed his knees and elbows, although the blood was dried on them now. "What's wrong?" I asked him.

Adam beckoned me to come closer. The doctor stepped back as Adam whispered in my ear. "You've got to get me out of this place."

"Why? What's happened?"

"I think they're all in on it together," he whispered.

I stepped back and looked him straight in the eyes. I then realised that this wasn't Adam. Not the Adam I knew. I didn't want to take him home whilst he was in this state of mind, but I knew I needed to appease him somehow. "Okay, just wait here for me. I need to speak to someone to straighten things out."

"No, you can't trust them, any of them!" There was a sense of urgency in his voice now.

"I know," I said, as calmly as I could. "Don't worry, I know what I'm doing. Please just wait here."

I disappeared through the curtains and found the doctor at the nurses' station on the phone. I knew he was talking about Adam so I waited expectantly for him to finish his conversation. "The on call Psychiatrist is on his way and the duty AMHP," he explained to me, after he had replaced the receiver.

"What does that mean?" I asked, although I think I already had a suspicion.

"Your husband seems very confused and paranoid. I take it this is not normal for him?"

"No, it isn't," I replied. "He has a drink problem. That's why he was in hospital. He had a seizure and he was undergoing detox, but he discharged himself earlier against medical advice."

"Has he drunk anything since he discharged himself?"

"I have no idea, because I don't know where he went. He could have I suppose. He had money on him."

Just then one of the nurses came scuttling over to us. "Mr Reynolds has gone," she panted.

The doctor and I both looked at each other with panic in our eyes. "Okay, call security," he said and ask them to bring him back here if they can.

By the time Adam was found and persuaded to return to the department, the Psychiatrist and AMHP (who was in fact a Social Worker) were already waiting for him. Adam seemed even angrier and more paranoid than before. "You can't keep me here!" he shouted.

"They just want to talk to you," said one of the female nurses, soothingly, placing a reassuring hand on his arm.

"Get your fucking hands off me!" shouted Adam, forcefully shrugging the nurse off and nearly knocking her off her feet. Then suddenly he was on the ground, pinned face down by several male members of staff. I could hear a pathetic whimper coming from Adam as his face was squashed into the tiled floor. I turned my head away. "Is that absolutely necessary?" I said, my voice breaking as tears welled up in my eyes.

"Why don't you wait in the relatives' room," suggested one of the nurses.

"I think I will," I said, "if that's okay?" She led me into a smallish, rather sparse room, containing four comfy chairs, and then offered me a drink. "I'd love a cup of tea," I said, remembering I'd left the one I had made earlier on the coffee table at home.

As I held the cup to my lips, silent tears running down my face and into the hot steaming tea, I felt incredibly guilty knowing Adam was out there, tormented and scared. *Maybe I should have just taken him home*, I thought. *Maybe he would have been all right after a good night's sleep and after the medication was out of his system.*

It seemed an eternity before someone came back into the room to see me. It was the Psychiatrist and the Social Worker. "He's very paranoid," the Psychiatrist explained. "That's why we feel Adam needs to go into a Psychiatric hospital for an urgent assessment. In his current state of mind, he may be a danger to himself or others. We can also complete the detox programme whilst he is in there." Silently I nodded. "He hasn't got the capacity to agree at the moment, so we want to admit him under the Mental Health Act."

"You mean, section him, don't you?" I said.

"Yes. That's if you agree?"

I nodded again, having now resigned myself to the inevitable. "Where will he go?"

"That depends on where there's a bed available I'm afraid. We'll try to get him in somewhere close to home, but that may not be possible."

"What do I do now?"

"If I was you, I'd go home and get some rest," said the Social Worker. "We'll ring you as soon as we know anything more."

"Okay." I was glad to be given permission to leave. All I wanted to do now was get home.

CHAPTER TWENTY-EIGHT

By the time I got home, it was late and I was tired, but I couldn't sleep, turning the events of the day over and over in my head. I eventually did fall asleep however on the settee around four in the morning.

The next thing I knew, I was awoken by my phone which was right beside me. "Hello?" I must have sounded rather groggy.

"Is that Mrs Reynolds?" came a half familiar voice at the other end of the phone.

"Yes?"

"It's Sean Edwards, the Social Worker. Just to let you know Adam's been admitted to Black Friars in Cheadle."

"Where's Cheadle?" I asked, sitting up.

"It's in Manchester."

"Manchester!" I echoed. That was miles away.

"I'm sorry we couldn't find a bed any nearer, but hopefully he'll be transferred to somewhere closer to home in a few days. If you want to visit, you need to ring them beforehand. I'll give you their number, shall I?"

"Yes, please," I replied. "I just need to get a pen."

Once I'd found a pen, Sean reeled off the number. "It might be best to wait until tomorrow to visit, but that's up to you," he suggested.

"How is he?" I asked. "Do you know?"

"Well apparently he needed about six people to restrain him before they transported him, as he got very aggressive, and he had to have an injection. But I was told he's much more settled now."

"Okay, thank you."

I looked at the time on my mobile phone. It was ten minutes to seven. I decided to make a drink before I started making telephone calls. Apart from ringing the hospital, I needed to ring my boss to ask if I could have some time off at short notice. I knew I needed to ring Ben and John as well, although I put these phone calls off until the last minute.

My boss was surprisingly considerate, telling me to take as much time off as I needed. Just after I rang off, I then had a phone call from the Consultant Psychiatrist at the hospital, pre-empting my call to them. He had a foreign accent and a foreign sounding name. I had to ask him to repeat it three times, but still hadn't understood what he said, feeling too embarrassed to ask him to repeat it again. He was extremely interested in Adam however, asking me lots of questions about his history, how long he'd been drinking and what his health had been like. I felt a bit more positive when I came off the phone, as it seemed that this doctor really wanted to help Adam, whether Adam wanted the help himself or not. When I did finally phone Ben and John, they were both shocked at the news, but fortunately didn't seem to hold me responsible in the slightest.

The following day I drove to Manchester. What with the traffic, it took me nearly three hours to get there. What I didn't realise until I arrived was that Adam was in a maximum-security wing of the hospital. I handed over my handbag which was placed in a locker, and they gave me a panic alarm before unlocking one of the heavy metal doors into the visitors' area. Adam was sat alone at one of the tables in a room that had the appearance of a prison visiting room rather than a hospital. "Will you be okay?" asked the male nurse before leaving.

"Yeah, I'll be fine," I replied. I sat down beside Adam in a rather uncomfortable hard plastic chair. He could barely lift his head to look at me, a trail of saliva running down his chin from his mouth.

"Hi, Fay," he said, almost in a whisper.

"How are you?" I asked, trying not to betray my shock at his appearance.

"I'm okay," he slurred. "Just really tired."

Adam crossed his arms on the table and I placed a comforting hand on his. "Well, you'll be back home before you know it. You just need to let them get you better first."

Adam nodded, without looking at me. We continued to engage in small talk for a while, although the conversation felt rather forced and stilted. I was somewhat relieved when the male nurse who I had seen earlier entered the room, asking us if we wanted a cup of tea. We were both appreciative of the offer and when the nurse returned with our tea and a plateful of biscuits, I took the opportunity of remarking on Adam's appearance. "I'm a bit concerned," I said, "Adam seems rather over sedated."

"It's just while he's going through detox," the nurse reassured me. "We'll be gradually reducing the dose over the next few days."

"Okay," I said, assuming that they must know what they're doing.

By the time I started to head back home, it was getting dark. Then it began to rain. A few random drops swiftly turned into a heavy shower that pelted the windscreen as the wipers frantically tried to clear it. As I grasped the steering wheel in both hands, the motorway stretching out before me, so straight and resolute, suddenly a song came on the radio, a song I instantly recognised. It was the song we had chosen for the first dance at our wedding all those years ago. Tears welled up in my eyes and as they began to roll down my cheeks, like hot and salty rivulets, the bright lights of the motorway splintered into a thousand shards of blinding light.

Once I started crying, I couldn't stop, barely able to see the road before me. The pain was almost too much to bear as I felt my heart breaking and being rend apart. This was a nightmare, a nightmare I couldn't wake up from.

CHAPTER TWENTY-NINE

Adam was in hospital for eight days. The seizures had fortunately not caused any brain damage. He was now completely off the Librium which helped him withdraw from the alcohol safely, and he was pretty much back to his usual self. He was discharged with some advice and written information about local A.A. groups and the Substance misuse service. After some persuasion, Adam agreed to attend his first A.A. meeting, providing I went along with him for support.

It was a Monday evening. As I parked the car, we could see people already making their way into the church hall. We went in together. At first Adam and I both just stood there like a couple of spare parts. Then someone came over to us. "Is this your first time here?" the middle-aged man asked. He had a friendly face.

"Yes," I replied. "This is Adam and I'm his wife, Fay. I've just come along to support him, if that's okay?"

"You're very welcome, both of you," said the man. "My name's Kenny."

"Pleased to meet you," I said.

"Yeah, pleased to meet you," Adam mumbled. Adam looked uncomfortable.

"Help yourself to coffee and cake," said Kenny, gesturing towards a table laden with two large coffee pots and an assorted collection of mugs, as well as a large sponge cake and some paper plates.

A couple of other people came over to us to introduce themselves as I poured the coffee.

"They all seem very friendly," I said, encouragingly.

A few minutes later, everyone sat down around a large table.

"Can we all hold hands now to begin the meeting with the Serenity Prayer," said Kenny.

All ten or so people around the table linked hands and recited, "God grant me the serenity to accept the things I cannot change; the courage to change the things I can; and the wisdom to know the difference."

I glanced sideways at Adam whose expression indicated he was not impressed. In fact I half expected him to get up there and then and leave. But he didn't.

"Tom, would you like to do the readings this evening?" said Kenny.

Tom nodded and then announced, "I'm Tom and I'm an alcoholic." He then proceeded to read the 12 steps. I glanced at Adam again as the word God was mentioned several times in the reading."

"Thank you, Tom," said Kenny. "Now I would like us to welcome a newcomer, Adam, and his wife, Fay who is here to support him at his first meeting."

"Welcome Adam and Fay," was the unified response.

"I would also like to congratulate Emma on reaching her fifth birthday and to thank her for bringing in the lovely cake. I'm sure you'll all agree it's delicious." Everyone clapped. Initially I was a little confused. Emma looked very young but was clearly a lot older than five. I then realised that her birthday marked the day she stopped drinking.

"I'd like to thank you all for supporting me over the past five years," said Emma. Emma was very pretty, slim with long red hair. It was hard to believe that she had ever had a drink problem. "I started drinking when I was only twelve years old," she continued. "By the time I was fifteen I was pregnant and had dropped out of school. I lost the baby as I couldn't stop drinking. I didn't care about my unborn child. All I cared about was where my next drink was coming from. It wasn't until I was able to surrender myself to a higher power that I was able to turn my life around."

"Thank you for sharing," said Kenny. "Would anyone else like to share?"

"I'm George," stated an older man, probably around sixty, "and I'm an alcoholic." His head was crowned with a mop of course grey hair, but he looked very respectable in his polo shirt and light brown chinos. "I always believed that you had to drink too much to have a drink problem. So as far as I was concerned, I didn't have a drink problem. Because you see, I could never drink enough." A ripple of laughter spread through the room and immediately I felt my tensed body relax a little. George then proceeded to tell us how he had lost everything; his wife, his children, his home and his job, because of the drink. "When I came home, my wife and kids would have to make sure they were out of my way, or else they'd get it. I was a real nasty piece of work. Eventually they left me. Because I'd lost my job and couldn't pay the bills, I ended up on the streets. Any money I did have I just spent on drink. Occasionally I'd end up in hospital. They'd feed me, wash my clothes which were usually covered in piss or vomit, I'd dry out and then they'd let me go again. And sure enough I'd go straight back on the booze. It wasn't until I started coming to meetings that I realised I had to stop blaming other people for the way things had turned out and start taking responsibility for my own actions." George was looking straight at Adam now. "You've taken the first step by being here, Adam. You're lucky your wife is still with you, supporting you."

I glanced at Adam. I was relieved to see he was nodding in agreement.

After we heard a few more stories, the meeting came to an end. Whilst I had been listening to their stories, I began to realise that this was probably the only place these people could be completely honest with others, as well as with themselves, because no one here would judge them, because they were all in the same boat. After the meeting a few people remained chatting informally for a while. Just about everyone congratulated Adam for taking the first step by attending the meeting. A couple of people even gave him their telephone numbers, explaining he could ring them at any time he had a craving. "Will we see you again at the next meeting?" asked one of them.

"Yeah, sure," said Adam, although I wondered whether he actually meant it.

CHAPTER THIRTY

Adam did continue to attend A.A. meetings. I gave him as much encouragement as I could, continually telling him how proud I was of him. He didn't tell me much about what went on, but he did tell me that he was now contributing himself, which seemed to be a massive step for him. I was getting increasingly worried about him however. He was starting to have problems at work. He claimed he was being victimised. He lost his appetite and more and more in the evenings I ate alone. He claimed he was unable to sleep at night and therefore by the morning felt unwell and exhausted. Sometimes the first thing he would do when he got out of bed was to rush to the bathroom to vomit. He would be noticeably shaking and would break out into a cold sweat. On a number of occasions I accused him of drinking but he insisted he hadn't been. I never saw him drink so I convinced myself that there must be something else wrong with him. "I think my symptoms are partly due to anxiety," Adam would offer as an explanation.

"You need to see a doctor," I said, on more than one occasion. "It's not normal to keep feeling so ill all the time, and you look awful."

Eventually Adam agreed to see a doctor. Or rather, he had no choice. He'd been off sick from work for a week already for which he had self-certificated. He did not feel well enough to return to work therefore would now need a doctor's note. He was given a sick note for two weeks due to the rather vague diagnosis of 'viral illness'.

It was eleven o'clock, Saturday morning. Adam had gone back to bed and I had started to clean out the kitchen cupboards. It was one of those jobs I had been putting off for a long time; one of those jobs not included in any job description I had been given, but somehow felt compelled to undertake by virtue of my sex. It was during this gratifying activity that I found something unexpected hidden behind the cans of baked beans. I picked it up and stared at it, initially in bewilderment. It was a half bottle of rum. Then as realisation dawned, my heart grew so heavy, I felt it fall to my feet like a stone.

When Adam eventually got up again, I presented him with the bottle of rum. "What's this?" I asked him.

Initially Adam said nothing, as he stared at me with a blank expression. "I must have put that there when I was still drinking," he explained eventually. "I forgot it was there."

"I wish I could believe that."

"It's the truth, honestly."

"Honestly?" I retorted sarcastically. "I don't think you know the meaning of that word." I wanted desperately for Adam to prove to me that he was telling the truth. But he couldn't. I only had his word. "Have you actually been going to the A.A. meetings all this time?"

"Of course I have."

"I really wish I could believe you." My tone of voice was calmer now, more resigned.

"Look, "began Adam, taking the bottle from me. "I'm pouring this down the sink." And he proceeded to do just that.

"A bold gesture," I said. "But it means very little. You'll just go out and buy another bottle anyway."

"What can I do?"

"Just tell me the truth. I'd respect you more if you just told me the truth."

Adam looked down at his feet, then drew a deep breath. "Okay," he said, looking up at me. "I'll tell you the truth."

I braced myself. I think part of me didn't even want to know the truth. Part of me wanted to be blissfully ignorant.

"I *have* been drinking. I just can't stop it all together. But with your support, I'm sure I can keep it under control."

I said nothing. Instead I turned and walked out of the kitchen.

"Where are you going?" asked Adam, as he followed me into the hallway.

"I need to go for a drive," I said, picking up my keys.

"Why?"

"I need to think."

I got into the car and turned the key in the ignition. I backed off the drive, barely checking behind me, turned the car around and drove up the road faster than I should have. My stomach was in knots. I wanted to burst into tears but I held them back. I didn't know where I was going. I just knew I had to get away. I turned the corner out of our cul-de-sac. I drove until I ended up driving along a country road. After a while I pulled over into a layby and turned the engine off. I left the radio on and just sat with my eyes closed, trying to relax by breathing slowly and deeply. I opened my eyes to see someone walking past the car with their dog. They smiled at me through the window and I thought I detected a slightly perplexed look in their eyes. I realised they were probably wondering why I was just sat there. I smiled back, rather awkwardly.

My mobile phone then began to ring. It was Adam. I answered it abruptly. “Yes?”

“Where are you?” he asked.

“Nowhere,” was my nonsensical reply.

“Look, I’m sorry, Fay. I know I’ve let you down, yet again.”

He sounded very reasonable and a lot calmer than I was feeling. I felt guilty then. Was I really expecting too much of him?

“I’m coming now,” I said. “I’ll talk to you when I get back.”

I turned on the engine and drove back home.

∞

When I arrived home, Adam was stood at the window, waiting expectantly for me. As I entered the sitting room, he turned to face me. I gazed into his eyes in a vain attempt to understand what was going on his head, or his heart, but Adam remained silent and almost expressionless. “Okay, I’ve been thinking,” I said at last. “I’m prepared to meet you half-way.”

“I’m listening….”

“From now on, I won’t complain about you drinking…..providing you keep it under control.”

“Really?”

“Just promise me one thing.”

“What?”

“I want you to be honest with me…..no more lies.”

“Deal.”

CHAPTER THIRTY-ONE

Two months passed. I was just pegging out the washing in the garden when I heard the phone ringing from inside the house. "Whose that?" I muttered to myself.

"Hi, Fay?" came the voice at the other end of the phone. "How are you?" It was John.

"Oh, fine really, thank you."

"Is Adam there?"

"No, he's out I'm afraid," I replied.

"That's fine, don't worry. I wanted to speak to you anyway."

"Oh?"

"Well firstly I wanted to invite you both to James and Christina's wedding."

"They're getting married at last? That's wonderful news!" I said. James and Christina had probably been together for five years already and no one doubted for one minute that they were meant for each other. "We'd love to come. When is it?"

"Not until Augu," John replied. "You'll get the formal invitation in the post."

"What was the other thing you wanted to speak to me about?"

"Well, I'm not sure how to put this, but I'm a bit concerned about Adam. I know he claims to have cut down on the booze, but ......"

"But?"

"I have some very strange conversations with him sometimes."

"What do you mean?"

"Well, I find he's constantly repeating himself. Telling me the same thing over and over again. I didn't think much of it at first, but he honestly seems to have no recollection of our previous conversations."

"Really?"

"Yes, really. For example, I already told Adam about the wedding the day before yesterday. He said he'd ask you and then ring me back, but he never did. And judging by your reaction when I just told you the news, he never mentioned it to you at all."

"No, he didn't." I was silent for a moment. "To be honest, John, I've been a bit worried too. I suppose I just didn't want to admit it to myself."

"I don't know if it's just because he's depressed. I know he's been having problems at work."

"Yeah," I said, "ever since he got this new manager. He seems to think he's got it in for him."

"Don't you think that sounds a bit paranoid?"
"It does I suppose. A bit."

We were now both silent for a moment. "Shall I get Adam to give you a ring when he comes in?" I asked, changing the subject.

"Yeah, you can do," replied John. "I wouldn't mention what we've been talking about to him though. He'll only get defensive."

"No, I won't," I assured him.

∞

When Adam arrived home later that day, I could tell he'd had more to drink than usual. I refrained from giving him a hard time however as he had received some very sad news. An old friend of his from school had died quite suddenly after a short illness, only the same age as Adam. Adam hadn't seen him for a while and didn't even know he was ill. I know he felt guilty about that, but I told him he shouldn't do. "I should have kept in touch," said Adam. "The last time we met up, I said I'd give him a ring to meet up again, but I never did."

"You wasn't to know," I said. "Everybody loses touch with people from time to time. That's life."

"But Graham was a good friend to me," said Adam. "I shouldn't have lost touch with him." There seemed to be no consoling him.

"John rang earlier," I said, trying to lighten the mood..

"Really?" replied Adam. "What did he want?"

"He wanted to invite us to James and Christina's wedding in August."

"They're getting married?" said Adam, genuinely surprised. "That's good news."

"Yes, it is isn't it?"

Adam looked rather solemn again. "I'll ring John tomorrow," he said.

CHAPTER THIRTY-TWO

Adam took the afternoon off work to go to the funeral. I would have gone with him, even though I didn't really know Graham that well, but I was very busy at work and there were already two people off in my office. Adam had said he wasn't sure whether or not he would stay for the wake, but he obviously had, judging by the time he got home. I was already home from work when I heard his car pull up outside. I looked out the window to see Adam getting out of the driver's seat. He had told me he would drive so that he wouldn't be tempted to drink too much. However as I watched him stagger up the path to the house, it was obvious he was well over the limit. I opened the front door just as he reached it and he promptly fell through the doorway, almost knocking me over in the process.

"I can't believe you drove home in this state!" I berated Adam, who was now on his hands and knees on the floor. "What were you thinking?" I deliberately refused to help him up.

"I'm okay," said Adam, slurring his words.

"Okay?" I exclaimed. "You think you're okay? You can barely stand up!"

Eventually Adam managed to get back on his feet. "I'm going to bed," he said, attempting to climb the stairs. I followed up behind him for fear that he would fall, although at the same time thinking, *it'll serve him right if he does!*

I didn't see Adam for the rest of the night. I could hear him snoring loudly as I climbed the stairs to bed later that evening. So I decided to sleep in the spare room, and not for the first time.

∞

Adam woke me the following morning when he came into my room with a mug of hot tea. He placed it on the bedside table. "Good morning, sleepy head," he said. He was remarkably bright and breezy considering the state he was in the evening before.

"What time is it?" I asked, sitting up in bed.

"It's about ten o'clock," said Adam. "Why did you sleep in here? Was I snoring again?"

"Yes," I retorted. What I didn't tell him was that I actually preferred sleeping alone anyway. We hadn't been intimate for a long time, partly because Adam was usually too drunk and partly because I could no longer bear his touch. At one time I never would have believed I could ever feel that way about him.

After I'd drunk my tea, I got up, had a shower and got ready to go out. I was meeting Jayne for brunch, as we called it, at 11.30. I came downstairs where Adam was watching the T.V. "Where are you going?" Adam asked as he watched me slip on my ankle boots and leather jacket.

"I'm meeting Jayne," I said.

"What time will you be back?"

"I don't know," I said. "Around three probably. We're going shopping after we've eaten."

"Okay, I'll see you later then," said Adam.

"See you later." Then just as I was walking out the door, I turned my head and said, "by the way, if you ever drink and drive again, I'll call the police. You could have killed someone. Maybe a child.....like Jessica or Emily."

∞

"How's Adam?" asked Jayne, as she tucked into her jacket potato.

I hesitated. I was going to tell her about his antics the evening before, but then I thought better of it. For some reason, I felt more embarrassed about his behaviour than he probably did himself. Particularly as I had told Jayne the last time I had seen her that Adam was doing so well. Or so I thought at the time. "He's doing okay," I said. "He's been a bit down lately though. He's got a new boss and they haven't been seeing eye to eye. Also an old friend of Adam's died suddenly, which didn't help matters. Adam was pretty cut up about it."

"Oh dear, I'm sorry to hear that."

"Yeah, the funeral was yesterday."

Jayne was silent for a moment. She seemed pensive. Then she spoke. "Mike and I are planning to get tickets for a play at The Empire.....*To kill a mocking bird.* We were wondering if you and Adam would like to come? We thought we'd go for a meal first. It was Mike's idea. He hasn't seen Adam for such a long time. What do you think?"

I thought for a moment. "Yeah, it sounds like a nice idea. Adam and I haven't been out together for a while. I'll ask him when I get home, but I'm sure he'll say yes. When is it?"

"The 17th of June. It's a Sunday, I'm afraid, but it shouldn't be a particularly late night."

"How much are the tickets?"

"Just under thirty pounds each."

"That's fine. I'll look forward to it," I said, smiling.

CHAPTER THIRTY-THREE

I had considered cancelling our night out with Jayne and Mike on more than one occasion, as Adam's drinking just seemed to be getting more and more out of control. He hadn't been at work for weeks, his doctor having signed him off again with yet another vague diagnosis. But we'd already bought the tickets and I'd hoped that spending time with our friends would be the tonic he needed. Adam had been withdrawing further and further into his shell, and it was almost becoming easier just to let him.

Mike and Jayne picked us up at five o'clock. It was about a twenty minute drive. Once Mike had parked the car, we followed him and Jayne to the Italian restaurant which was situated just around the corner. "This seems a nice place," I remarked as we entered the restaurant.

A smart, Italian looking waiter dressed in a white shirt, with a black waistcoat and trousers, approached us. "Do you have a reservation?"

"Yes," replied Mike. "In the name of Templeman."

We were then directed to a circular table in the far corner of the room. It was already laid for four people, with a crisp white tablecloth, and serviettes folded inside crystal clear wine glasses. In the centre of the table stood a bud vase containing a single red rose and next to it, a votive candle flickered in its glass holder.

"Would you like an aperitif?" asked the waiter.

"I think I'll have a champagne cocktail," said Jayne.

"That sounds nice," I said.

"Yeah, they're lovely," said Jayne. "A bit expensive, but I think you have to push the boat out occasionally, don't you?"

"Yeah, you're right," I said. "I think I'll have one of those as well."

"I'm just gonna have a beer," said Mike. "Don't worry, I'll be on the soft drinks after that," he reassured Jayne.

"It's a shame you can't drink, Mike," I said.

"It's okay. It doesn't bother me really," said Mike. "I like to keep a clear head anyway."

"I'll have a beer as well," said Adam.

"I'll come back for your food order in a few minutes," said the waiter, and then he left.

"Ooh, I'm spoilt for choice," I said as I scanned the menu. "What are you having, Adam?"

"I don't know," he replied. "I might just have a bolognaise."

A few minutes later the waiter returned with our drinks. "Are you ready to order your meals?"

"Yes, I think so," said Jayne. We all nodded in agreement.

"Would any of you like starters?" the waiter asked.

"No, thank you," we all said in unison.

"So, what would you like for the main course?"

"I'll have the lasagne," said Jayne. "And can I have garlic bread with that, please?"

"Of course, Madam."

"I'll have the cannelloni," said Mike.

"And would you also like the garlic bread with that, Sir?"

"Yes, please," replied Mike.

Adam ordered the spaghetti bolognaise and I ordered the chicken cacciatore.

"Could I also order a bottle of house red?" asked Adam. I immediately felt my stomach muscles tighten. Adam knew I didn't like red wine and Mike wouldn't be drinking anything else, so unless Adam was contemplating sharing it with Jayne, which I doubted, he planned to drink the entire bottle of red wine himself.

"Do you fancy sharing a bottle of white or rose?" I asked Jayne, figuring if you can't beat him, join him.

"Yeah, go on then," said Jayne, although I'm not sure how much I can drink.

"Cheers!" we all said in unison, as we clinked glasses. I then noticed that as Adam brought his glass to his lips, his hand was shaking. I wondered if Mike or Jayne had also noticed.

"How's things going with you Adam?" asked Mike, as he placed his glass back carefully on the table.

"Well, they could be better," Adam replied. "I've got this new boss. I just can't get on with him. In fact he seems determined to make my life hell."

"Oh dear, sorry to hear that," said Mike. "The last time I saw you, you seemed to be enjoying your job."

"I was," replied Adam. "But not now. I'm actually off work with stress at the moment."

"Really? That bad?" said Mike.

"Yeah, it's that bad," said Adam, sullenly. "In fact, more than once I've thought about just walking out."

"Well, you're not going to, are you, Adam?" I said, raising the pitch of my voice in an attempt to conceal the seriousness of my warning. "I can't afford to support us both on my wages."

There was an awkward silence for what seemed a long time, but was probably only a few moments. "How's Ben?" asked Jayne, breezily.

"He's doing fine," I replied, grateful to her for changing the subject. "Although we don't see him as much as we'd like to."

"How old are his girls now?" asked Mike.

"They're about three and five, aren't they?" said Adam.

"No. They're six, both of them, because they're twins, remember?" I said curtly, rolling my eyes.

"Oh, of course," said Adam, "I forget."

I noticed Jayne and Mike throw one another disconcerted glances

"How's Sarah?" I asked.

"She's fine," said Jayne. "Nathan's a lovely lad, isn't he, Mike?"

"Yeah, top bloke," said Mike. "We're just waiting for them to give us some grandchildren now." Mike was a real family man. For him, kids would always come first. He and Adam were unalike in that respect, for where Adam was concerned, where his next drink was coming from was always priority in his mind, even though he would probably deny this vehemently.

"Remember when Sarah and Ben were little?" I said. "They were inseparable. Almost like brother and sister."

"Yeah, I feel it's a shame sometimes they have to grow up," said Jayne.

A few minutes later our meals arrived, followed by the wine. The food was delicious but I couldn't completely relax, even after a couple of glasses of wine. Adam's hands were no longer shaking, but he seemed to be knocking his wine back far too quickly, although he had barely touched his meal.

"I was sorry to hear you lost a friend recently," said Mike. "Was it anyone I knew?"

"I don't think so," said Adam. "His name was Graham Foster."

"No, I don't recognise the name," said Mike. "How old was he?"

"The same age as me," said Adam.

"That's no age at all, is it?" said Mike.

"No, it isn't," said Adam. "And he was a good bloke. Didn't deserve to be taken so young." Adam's voice began to quiver as he broke down in tears. Mike and Jayne were both looking at me with anxious expressions on their faces. Graham's death was undoubtedly very sad but even so, Adam's public display of grief seemed inappropriate somehow. It wasn't as if Adam and Graham had been that close, at least not over the past few years.

Fortunately Adam managed to pull himself together quite quickly and a few moments later, his mood had changed again completely. He was smiling and joking, seemingly without a care in the world, his eyes still wet with tears.

When we arrived at the theatre, we just had enough time to place an order for drinks at half-time. We then took our seats and waited for the play to commence. Jayne and Mike had managed to get us pretty decent seats, in the dress circle, with a good view of the stage.

When the lights rose in the auditorium for the intermission, we made our way to the bar. We had all ordered soft drinks apart from Adam, who had ordered a large glass of red wine. Before long an anonymous voice announced the start of the second half of the play, barely giving us enough time to finish our drinks. "I need a pee," said Adam, "so I'll see you in there in a minute."

"Don't be long then," I said. "It's just about to start."

We took our seats, the lights dimmed once again and the curtain went up. Adam still hadn't returned. "Do you think Adam's okay?" whispered Jayne. "Shall I ask Mike to go look for him?"

"No, it's okay," I whispered in reply. "I'm sure he's fine."

After what seemed like hours, I became aware of a disturbance in the auditorium. At first I couldn't see what or who was causing it. Then I noticed people standing up several rows in front of us. Someone was trying to make their way back to their seat. Suddenly I realised it was Adam.

"Adam! Adam!" I called out, in as loud a whisper as I could manage. "We're over here!" But he didn't seem to hear me. I could practically feel my blood pressure rising. People were now turning their heads with frowns etched on their faces, and I could hear exasperated sighs and tuts from all around me. Someone must have alerted Adam to the fact that I was trying to attract his attention, because he then turned around and started to make his way up the steps towards us. He stumbled in the semi-darkness, landing flat on his face. Fortunately a kind and considerate gentleman left his seat to help Adam up. Adam eventually reached our row. People began to stand up rather begrudgingly to allow Adam to pass. Finally he plonked himself down in the seat between me and Jayne. "Sorry," Adam muttered, but I said nothing. My silence encapsulated every bit of anger and disappointment that was simmering within me.

I did wonder where Adam had been all this time. *Probably went back to the bar*, I thought to myself. I was just beginning to relax and continue watching the play when I heard a deep rumbling sound. I looked at Adam. His chin was almost touching his chest and he was snoring. I gently shook him but his head just lolled about and he continued to snore, and it seemed to be getting louder. I began to pinch his thigh as hard as I could in an attempt to rouse him, but he was obviously in such a deep state of insensibility that it had no effect. Centuries seemed to pass. The play ended. The cast took their bows and the audience applauded. The auditorium was once again illuminated so that I could clearly see a host of disapproving and disgruntled expressions directed towards me and Adam. I felt like announcing, *I'm not responsible for him. For this. I'm as annoyed as you are, probably more, believe me. You're the lucky ones. You can go home and leave him behind. Not me!*

Eventually I managed to rouse Adam and get him to his feet. We all said very little on our way back to the car. I linked my arm in Adam's. Not out of any affection for him, but purely to prevent him from falling over and embarrassing me yet again.

CHAPTER THIRTY-FOUR

I had arranged to take the following two days off work. On the Monday, Adam didn't get up until almost lunchtime, and then spent the afternoon in his dressing gown. We hardly spoke until the evening. Adam must have realised I was still annoyed with him as he seemed to be treading on egg shells around me. I never noticed him drink until the evening either, and then he seemed to drink very little in comparison to the evening before.

On the Tuesday I was awoken by the sound of someone throwing their guts up in the bathroom. I checked the time on my mobile phone, which was on the bedside cupboard. It was a quarter past eight.

A few minutes later Adam came back to bed. He pulled the duvet up to his chin. He was trembling. His face was pale and a sheen of sweat had broken out on his forehead. "What's the matter?" I asked, trying not to sound too concerned. I was still a little angry with him.

"I don't know," said Adam. Even his voice was shaking. "I think I must have flu, or something."

I got out of bed myself and put on my dressing gown. "I'm going to make myself a cup of tea," I said. "Do you want one? Or coffee?"

"No thanks," said Adam. "I'd like a glass of water though."

"Okay."

I padded downstairs and into the kitchen. I poured a glass of water for Adam and carried it upstairs while the kettle boiled.

"Thanks, darling," said Adam, as I handed him the glass of water.

"I'll be downstairs if you need me," I said.

"You not coming back to bed?"

"No," I replied. "I'll pop up in a bit to see you."

Adam was in bed most of the day. He couldn't keep anything down and he continued to shake. In fact the shaking became so violent that he could barely walk to the bathroom. I began to wonder if what he was experiencing was withdrawal again, not flu. He'd drunk so much on Sunday and then very little the following day; I was quite sure of that. I had previously read somewhere that a sudden reduction in alcohol intake can trigger acute symptoms of withdrawal, not just sudden abstinence. I was getting increasingly concerned that Adam would have another seizure, so I rang the surgery. After a rather awkward discussion with the receptionist, she agreed to put me through to the duty doctor, Dr Campbell. "He's shaking so badly now, I'm afraid he's going to have another seizure," I explained.

"What he needs is alcohol," said Dr Campbell. "He mustn't stop drinking abruptly."

"I know that," I said, "but he can barely keep water down, let alone anything else. Isn't there something you can give him to help him with the withdrawal?"

"I'll prescribe some diazepam," said Dr Campbell. "I'll do the prescription now, so if you can pop down to the surgery, I'll leave it at the front desk for you."

"Thank you," I said, relieved.

"I will need to see Adam before the end of the week though," said Dr Campbell. "When you come down, ask the receptionist to book an appointment for him. Tell her I said he needs to be fitted in urgently."

I drove down to the surgery faster than I should have. Fortunately I found somewhere to park straight away. I collected the prescription and managed to get Adam an appointment with Dr Campbell for the Friday. I then took the prescription into the pharmacy next door.

When I got back home, Adam had somehow managed to make his way downstairs. I went into the kitchen and poured him a fresh glass of water. "Here, take this," I said, handing him one of the tablets. Adam dutifully swallowed the tablet with a gulp of the water. "Let's just hope you manage to keep that down."

Fortunately he did, and the shaking almost subsided. I gave him another tablet four hours later.

By the morning, Adam seemed to be feeling much better. I was tempted however to ring my boss to ask her if I could take another day off. "I'll be all right," Adam reassured me. "You go to work."

"Okay," I acquiesced. "Dr Campbell recommended you carry on taking the diazepam until you see him, even if you don't think you need it. As long as you don't drink."

"I won't drink," said Adam. "I promise you. I don't even feel like a drink."

I smiled. Adam seemed sincere. Maybe this time he would do it. Maybe this time he would uphold his promise. Now that he had some medication.

CHAPTER THIRTY-FIVE

It was Wednesday. I had only been at work for about an hour when Adam rang me on my mobile. "Hi, what is it?" I asked. "Are you okay?"

"Yes, I'm fine," replied Adam. "What you doing?"

"I'm at work," I replied, rather impatiently. "Have you rang me for any particular reason?"

"No," said Adam. "I just wanted someone to talk to. I'm feeling really fed up."

I sighed heavily. "I'm a bit busy," I said. "Why don't you give John a ring?"

"Okay."

Half an hour later, Adam was ringing me again. This time I ignored it. But Adam didn't get the message as he kept ringing me over and over again. So, rather guiltily, I switched my phone to silent. Eventually he stopped ringing me. And then I began to worry. I even ended up by ringing him, believing there must be something wrong. Really wrong. But he didn't answer.

When I arrived home at around 5.30, the house was in silence. Adam wasn't downstairs. I climbed the stairs and found him asleep in bed. I went back downstairs to the kitchen. I filled the kettle and switched it on.

I left Adam to sleep. I made myself some tea. Just scrambled eggs on toast. I wasn't in the mood for cooking much, especially just for myself. After I washed up, I returned to the sitting room to watch some television. Just as I was thinking of going to bed, I heard Adam on the stairs. He then appeared in the doorway.

"You're up early," he said.

"What time do you think it is?" I asked.

Adam stepped into the room, and glanced over at the clock on the mantelpiece. "It's ten thirty," he said. "I thought it was earlier than that."

"is it ten thirty in the morning or the evening?" I asked, testing him.

Adam fixed his gaze on me now. He looked lost, confused, almost like a small child. "The morning," he replied.

"Look outside," I said.

Adam walked over to the window and drew back one of the curtains. "Oh. It's dark. It must be evening. My sleep pattern's all over the place."

"You've not been taking more Diazepam than you should, have you?" I asked.

"No." Adam's tone was abrupt.

"And you've not been drinking?"

"No, of course not," said Adam. He sounded indignant.

"Well, I'm going to bed now," I said, standing up.

"Oh no, stay up with me for a bit, won't you?"

"Some of us have to work in the morning," I said, sarcastically. "Don't have the tele too loud, will you?" And with that, I left the room.

I took a long time to settle off to sleep. I might as well have stayed up for a while longer, I thought. I don't know why I felt sorry for Adam sitting downstairs watching tele on his own, but I did.

Eventually I fell asleep and when I woke up the next morning, Adam was in bed next to me. By the time I left for work, he was awake, so I said goodbye to him as I gave him some parting advice. "Try not to spend all day in bed."

∞

I was quite surprised to find Adam up and dressed when I arrived home from work. He was in the kitchen, stirring the contents of a large saucepan which was on the hob. "What are you cooking?" I asked him.

"Chilli."

"Oh, nice." I always liked Adam's chilli. "Have I got time to take Susie for a walk?"

"Yeah," replied Adam, "it won't be ready for a while yet."

It was a nice evening, so I decided to take Susie to the park where I could let her loose. As soon as I unclipped the lead from her collar, she began racing around in ever increasing circles, until she was barely visible by the light of the setting sun. I called out to her and within a couple of seconds, she was racing back towards me. Eventually she laid down in the long grass, panting, her long pink tongue hanging out of her open mouth. Obediently, she waited unmoving, watching me as I approached her, until I had fastened the lead to her collar.

As we made our way back home, my mouth began watering and my stomach growled in anticipation of Adam's chilli.

When I opened the front door, I was greeted by the smell of chilli, but also by the smell of something burning. I followed Susie into the kitchen, walking past the open door to the sitting room where Adam was half-sitting, half-lying on the settee, snoring. Susie emitted a soft whine as she came face to face with the strange beast on the hob, the contents of its belly oozing out from under its lid, that jiggled about erratically, running down the outside of its steel body, hissing and spitting as it hit the hot plate underneath.

I swiftly turned off the hob, grabbed an oven glove and then the handle of the pan, sliding it across to one of the other plates. Susie looked up at me with her big brown eyes, as if to say, *have you killed it now, mummy?* I then opened a window. I was surprised that it hadn't set off the fire detector. I made a mental note to check that it was still working properly.

I filled one of Susie's bowls with cold water from the tap and placed it on the linoleum floor. Thirstily she lapped it up. I then took out one of the tins of meat from the cupboard under the sink and opened it. She still had some biscuits in her other bowl so I added the meat to it. I then switched on the kettle to make myself a cup of coffee. I had been looking forward to the chilli, but I had lost my appetite now.

∞

I don't think Adam came to bed at all that night and as far as I know, he hadn't eaten anything either. When I got up for work the following morning, Adam was asleep on the settee, still fully clothed. A faint but distinct odour of stale sweat emanated from him, and he needed a shave. Considering he had stopped drinking, he seemed to be going downhill fast.

I managed to rouse Adam before I left. "Don't forget your Doctor's appointment this afternoon, will you?"

"No, I won't," replied Adam, sleepily.

"And make sure you get yourself cleaned up first."

I didn't hear from Adam all day and as I was driving home from work, I had this uneasy feeling that Adam had missed his Doctor's appointment. I intended to ring him beforehand to remind him but it got so busy at work, I didn't have the time. Perhaps I should have tried to get the time off work to go with him. Perhaps he shouldn't have been going there on his own at all. I suddenly realised that I was now feeling guilty. Responsible somehow. Somewhere along the way, I'd become more than just his wife.

When I arrived home, I noticed the curtains in the bedroom and sitting room were still drawn. Realising the house was in silence, I walked into the sitting room. Adam wasn't there. What was there however was an empty can of super strength beer on the coffee table, with an empty strip of Diazepam. My heart sank. And then a feeling of panic rose swiftly up into my throat. He had been drinking after all, as well as taking the Diazepam. In fact he'd probably been drinking all along, or at least since I went back to work.

Then I noticed the photo frame on the mantlepiece was lying face down, an empty space beside it which the black Murano glass cat always occupied. As I approached the fireplace and reached out my hand to stand the photo frame back upright. I heard the sound and felt the sensation of something hard crunching under my feet. I looked down to see the floor glistening with a hundred shards of black glass.

I stooped down and carefully picked up one of the large fragments of glass and placed it in the palm of my hand. Then as I stared at what appeared to be the ear of a cat, a single teardrop, wet yet soft and warm against my skin, fell into the palm of my hand. With tears in my eyes, I made my way to the kitchen to collect the dustpan and brush, and then proceeded to sweep up what was left of the one thing my mother had given me that I had treasured most of my life.

I eventually climbed the stairs and found Adam in bed. "Adam! Adam!" He couldn't have been in a deep sleep because he opened his eyes. The whites of his eyes were bloodshot. "I need to talk to you."

"What about?" he asked, sleepily.

"I'm going back downstairs," I said. "Can you come down in a minute?"

"Okay." Adam closed his eyes again.

I let Susie in and then fed her. I turned on the kettle and began to make myself a cup of tea, and Adam a strong cup of coffee. I was just beginning to think that he must have gone back to sleep when he appeared in the doorway, barefooted, wearing his dressing gown. "I'll be through in a minute," I said. "I'm just making you a coffee."

"Thanks."

As I carried the steaming hot mugs into the sitting room, I noticed the empty can of beer and the strip of tablets were missing. Adam was sat on the settee staring ahead at some rubbish on the TV. I placed his mug on the coffee table in front of him. "Thanks," he said, without looking at me. I settled into the arm chair, still holding my cup, wondering where he had hidden the can and tablets.

"Would you mind turning that down for a minute?" I asked him.

Adam pressed the mute button on the TV control. "What is it?" he asked, glancing over at me.

"We can't go on like this," I said.

"Like what?"

"You lying to me all of the time for starters."

"What am I lying about?" he asked.

"Okay," I began. "Let's just see if you can tell me the truth for once." I left an appropriate pause. "Are you drinking at the moment?"

"No," replied Adam, emphatically. "Of course not."

"Then how come I found the glass cat my mother gave me smashed into smithereens on the floor?" Adam looked at me with a slightly perturbed expression. "You didn't even have the courtesy to sweep it up."

"I'm really sorry," said Adam, looking down shamefully. "It was an accident. I meant to sweep it up before you got home but I fell asleep."

I was silent for a moment. I don't know which I felt more: angry or upset. "But you're still taking the Diazepam, I take it?" I said at last.

"Yeah, one or two," said Adam. "I don't want to have another seizure."

I just looked down and shook my head, in disbelief.

"Why are you shaking your head?"

"Did you honestly think I hadn't seen the empty can of beer on the table?"

Adam heaved a great sigh. "Okay, okay, so you've rumbled me. I'll stop now."

"Like that's going to happen," I said sarcastically. "You're probably addicted to two things now."

"Look, I'm sorry. I had every intention of stopping. It's just really difficult, that's all."

"Did you even go to the Doctor's today?"

Adam was now sitting on the edge of the settee, leaning forward with his elbows resting on his knees. He looked down into his lap. "I didn't need to see the Doctor again," he replied. "I'm fine now."

"How can you say that?" I found myself shouting.

"Do you have to shout?" said Adam, who seemed surprisingly calm in the circumstances. Unlike me. I then realised I needed to stay in control, so I took a deep breath and tried to compose myself.

"Look, I realise that this must be difficult for you," I said in a much gentler tone of voice. "Which is why you need help. Professional help. I really think you need to go into rehab."

"I don't think that's necessary," said Adam.

"Well, put it this way," I began. "If you really want to stop drinking, you need to prove it to me by getting help. Otherwise, I will have to leave. So it's up to you. Make your choice." I wasn't messing around anymore.

"Do I really have to go into rehab?"

"No," I said. "It's your choice. But don't expect me to stick around any longer to witness you killing yourself. I have a choice too."

"Okay, okay," Adam acquiesced. "I'll go into rehab."

"Really?" i didn't expect him to agree to it so quickly.

"Yes, really," replied Adam. "I don't want to lose you."

I was relieved that Adam had agreed, although I think a part of me realised that it probably wasn't what he really wanted. That he had agreed to go into rehab purely to prevent me from leaving. I wanted to arrange something straight away before Adam changed his mind, but it was too late now. "I'll see what I can sort out first thing in the morning," I said. Adam nodded his head, and I wondered if he'd be so agreeable tomorrow. Realising he probably needed some encouragement, I said, "I'm proud of you, you know, for making this choice."

CHAPTER THIRTY-SIX

I searched through the drawer in the kitchen for one of the leaflets they had given to Adam when he left the hospital months before. It was the drawer that contained a collection of leaflets, receipts, product manuals, spare batteries, sellotape, envelopes and used jiffy bags that it seemed too wasteful to discard. At first I thought I must have thrown it away, or Adam had, but then I found it. I picked up the telephone receiver and dialled the number for the *Substance misuse team.* Someone answered after only a couple of rings which took me somewhat by surprise.

"Oh, hello, um...." I faltered. "I wonder if you can help me.....I'm ringing on behalf of my husband.....he has an alcohol problem...."

"Shall I put you through to one of the nurses?"

"Oh, yes, please, if you don't mind."

Then after a few seconds, "hello, my name's Angela; I'm one of the nurses. Can I help you?"

"Yes, I hope so....I'm ringing on behalf of my husband....he has an alcohol problem," I began again, rather hurriedly. "Well his drinking is really out of control now. He has at last agreed to accept help so I was wondering how he can get admitted to the detox unit?"

"Well, he would have to have a GP referral to start with," she explained, "after which I'm afraid he would have to go on a waiting list."

"How long would he have to wait?"

"Well after we receive the referral, it could be up to six weeks I'm afraid.... possibly longer. And that's only for the initial assessment. It's likely to be a lot longer before your husband gets a place in the detox unit."

"But I don't think he'll even last six weeks if he carries on the way he's been going!" I could feel my voice shaking. "And I really can't cope with this any longer...."

"I'm sorry." Angela's tone was gentle and in any other situation, may have been comforting.

"I just don't know what to do...." My voice trailed off. I knew I sounded helpless; utterly pathetic.

"Well, I'm afraid the only other option I can suggest is that you go private. There are a lot of very good private clinics out there and you may be able to get a place pretty much straight away. Also the patient can usually stay for as long as they like, depending on what you can afford, whereas we can only provide a maximum of two weeks residential care. After that, we only offer out-patient appointments, unless we manage to secure funding for one of the private rehab clinics. But I can't guarantee we'll be able to do that, I'm afraid."

Angela explained that she could not recommend any specific clinics, but she was able to direct me to certain reputable websites, so as soon as I thanked her and replaced the receiver, I turned on my laptop and started to search for private rehab clinics.

I found one that seemed perfect. *This elegant Georgian manor*, it read, *retains many of its original features and is set amidst beautiful landscaped gardens, providing a sense of tranquillity and well-being. Our single occupancy bedrooms are comfortable, yet stylish, all with en suite facilities. The therapeutic process revolves around the twelve-step abstinence-based philosophy and aims to minimise the physical and psychological distress of withdrawal by establishing abstinence in a safe and supportive environment.* I then clicked on *photo gallery* to view all of the photos. One could be forgiven for mistaking the place for a five star hotel rather than a clinic. As I dialled the telephone number on the website, I felt my stomach muscles tighten in anticipation.

"Hello, Green Acres, can I help you?"

"Oh, hello, I'm just enquiring about your availability."

"Is this for yourself?" asked the woman at the other end of the phone.

"No, for my husband."

She then asked me a series of questions about him, all of which would be immaterial if it turned out we couldn't afford the fees.

"We expect people to enrol in the programme for a minimum of 6 weeks," she explained.

"Do you have any vacancies?" I asked

"Yes we do as it happens. We have two rooms available at this present time."

"How much?" I asked, tentatively.

"It's three thousand pounds."

"In total?"

"No, it's three thousand a week."
"So that's eighteen thousand pounds in total.... minimum?" *Of course it is, you idiot, that's simple maths.*

"Yes, plus another two thousand for aftercare."

"Twenty thousand then?"

"Yes."

I emitted an extremely heavy sigh of disappointment. "Oh, no, that's far too much, we really haven't got that sort of money I'm afraid. Thank you anyway."

After a great deal of searching, I finally found a rehab clinic that seemed highly recommended without the fees being too astronomical. They had a vacancy and were willing to allow Adam to complete the programme in four weeks rather than the customary minimum of six. With some degree of reticence, Adam agreed to go, although I still hadn't figured out yet how we were going to pay for it. The clinic agreed to reserve a place until the Monday. Fortunately they agreed to forego the deposit on this occasion, providing I brought a cheque with me on Monday for the full amount.

Initially I tried contacting the bank. "I'm just ringing to ask for a top up on my loan," I explained.

"How much more do you wish to borrow?"

"An extra seven thousand....if that's possible."

"Could you tell me what it's for?"

What do I say? My husband needs to go into rehab because he's a fall down drunk? "Home improvements," I said, as nonchalantly as I could.

After a number of other questions and credit checks, the answer came back. "I'm afraid your request has been declined. Is there anything else we can help you with?"

"No. No, thank you," I sighed.

Okay, now for Plan B. Telephone John. John had always said I should contact him if I needed anything, if there was anything he could do to help.

"*How much*?" exclaimed John.

"I know it sounds like a lot but believe me, that's at the cheaper end of the market. It also includes aftercare." *I sound like a sales woman*. "And I promise we will pay you every penny back.....as soon as we can."

"I'm sorry, Fay," began John. "As much as I'd like to help you, I can't justify spending that sort of money, especially as I can't be sure that he'll stick it out anyway."

"That's okay. I understand. It *is* a lot of money."

I did understand, but I also felt disappointed, and deflated. I didn't think John would let me down. I didn't think he would let Adam down.

There was only one other person I could approach. I dialled his number, a number I knew by heart. "Hello," came the warm dulcet tone at the other end of the phone.

"Hi, Dad!" I said, casually. "Are you okay?"

"Yeah, I'm fine, darling. What can I do for you?" *What indeed.*

"I was wondering, could I pop up and see you....tonight. I just need to talk something over with you."

"Two visits in one week.... I am honoured! "

"That's if you've not got anything else on?"

"Wait a minute, I'll just check my social calendar," and then there was a pause. "Nope, nothing on tonight. Angelina Jolie has just cancelled."

I forced out a laugh. "Okay, Dad, I'll be with you in about an hour."

Dad lived about thirty five miles away which made it difficult to visit him as often as I would have liked. He moved back to his own home town about ten years ago. I'm not really sure why he did, and I knew a part of him always regretted it, particularly as we were living even further away from one another now. Today however I was glad for the long drive so that I could practice the conversation in my head I needed to have with him. It was raining when I arrived. He opened the front door as I was walking up the path, so that I wouldn't have to get too wet whilst waiting on the doorstep. "I've just put the kettle on," he said, as I entered the hallway and began taking off my jacket. "Do you want tea or coffee?"

Visiting Dad was always like coming home, no matter where his home might be. "A coffee would be lovely," I said, hanging up my jacket on one of the pegs in the hallway. Dad trotted off to the kitchen and I made my way into the lounge, sitting down on the sofa. A couple of minutes later, Dad appeared with a steaming mug in each hand.

"There you are," he said, placing the mug on the coffee table in front of me. He then sat down in the armchair adjacent to me, with his mug still in his hand. "Now what can I do for you?"

"Well, I wanted to ask you a favour," I began. "I won't be offended if you say no. After all, it's a lot to ask…."

"Just spit it out, darling."

"Well, I was wondering if you could lend me some money. I wouldn't ask if I wasn't desperate." I hated having to ask my dad for money. I was a grown up now and Dad was a pensioner. I felt that I should be the one helping him out now. I looked down at my hands which were resting in my lap. When I looked back up, Dad was wearing a perplexed, yet concerned expression.

"Can I ask you what it's for?"

"Adam's agreed to go to a private clinic for detox and rehab. I think now it's the only chance he's got." Over the past couple of years, I had struggled to keep Adam's secret, although I wouldn't have been surprised to discover that Dad in fact had held suspicions for much longer.

Dad was silent for a moment and then he asked "how much will it cost?"

"Seven thousand pounds," I replied. "That's for four weeks and includes aftercare."

Dad raised one eyebrow. Such was his composure, a raised eyebrow was the extent of his expression of surprise.

"Okay. I think I can manage that. Do you need it straight away?"

"I'm afraid so."

"Okay, I'll just get my cheque book."

∞

By the time I got home it was dark. I'd accidentally left my mobile phone at home and there were two missed calls from John and one from Adam, who was now asleep on the settee. I telephoned John but Jennifer answered. "Sorry, Fay but John's gone out."

"Do you know what he wanted?" I asked.

"I think he just wanted an update on the Adam situation." *The Adam situation?* Already I didn't much like her choice of words.

"Yeah, everything's gonna be fine. I've just got back from my Dad's. He's agreed to lend me the money for the clinic, so hopefully Adam will be admitted on Monday."

"Yeah John told me how much it was going to cost and I think it's admirable that you're prepared to put so much on the line to help him, but to be honest, Fay, the trouble with you is you're too soft. Don't get me wrong, John likes a drink, but he knows I wouldn't put up with the behaviour you put up with. I know it's probably none of my business, but I really think you should just put your foot down once and for all, Fay."

No, it isn't any of your business, but you're going to stick your nose in anyway, even though you haven't a fucking clue what you're talking about. "So you're saying it's *my* fault that he's an alcoholic?" I said, sarcastically.

"I wasn't saying that at all, Fay. "*Yes, you were.* I hated the way she liked to end her sentences with my name, so that it would sound like a reprimand. "Look, I've been reading up on alcoholism a lot lately," (*everyone's an expert)* "and I just think you should look at what you're doing as well, because despite your best intentions, you maybe just enabling his addiction. But then perhaps I don't know what I'm talking about." Her tone was sarcastic now.

"No you don't," I said, curtly. "It's one thing reading about it, but another thing actually living it." I never used to be this assertive with Jennifer but my stress levels were high and the last thing I needed was one more person to piss me off. I think buried underneath all the indignation though was some sense of realisation, realisation that to some degree, Jennifer was right.

CHAPTER THIRTY-SEVEN

We began to make our way to Oxfordshire, me in the driving seat, Adam sat beside me. "I wish I didn't have to go," he said.

"You're not having second thoughts, are you?" I asked.

"No. I said I'd go. I'll just really miss you that's all."

"It's only for four weeks," I said. "And after the first week, I'll visit you every weekend. And we can speak on the phone." We had been told that Adam could have no visitors or phone calls during the first week, although I could ring up to speak to the staff to check on his progress.

Half-way along our journey we stopped at the motorway services and both had a burger and fries. By the time we reached the clinic, I noticed that Adam was beginning to shake. The satnav led us off the main road and along a narrow lane, that opened out into a gravel drive. I parked the car and as we lifted Adam's bags out of the boot, a woman appeared in the doorway of what looked like a large country cottage rather than a clinic.

"Hello!" said the woman. "Is it Adam?"

"Yes," I replied for him.

"Pleased to meet you," she said, walking towards us and then shaking Adam's hand. "My name's June. I'm one of the senior therapists here." June then turned to face me. "And you must be Fay."

"Yes, that's right," I said.

"If you'd like to follow me, I'll fetch you some refreshments. Would you like tea or coffee?" Then when I was just about to reply, she added, "we also have juice or mineral water if you'd prefer?"

"Tea would be lovely, thank you," I said.

We followed June into the cottage and into a large sitting room off of the hallway. We dumped the bags on the floor and made ourselves comfortable on one of the black leather settees. Except Adam didn't look comfortable. He seemed restless and agitated.

"This is nice," I said, scanning the room. Apart from the two black settees, there was a large wooden coffee table placed in front of the fireplace, which was sandwiched between two bookcases containing a collection of books and DVDs. At the other end of the room stood a long imposing dining table surrounded by ten high leather back chairs.

A few minutes later June returned with a large tray laden with a pot of tea, milk jug, sugar bowl, cups and saucers and a plate of biscuits. She carefully placed the tray upon the coffee table and after asking us how we liked it, hospitably poured and handed us both a cup of tea. "Help yourselves to biscuits if you wish."

"Thank you," I said, reaching out for one of the digestives. Adam didn't take a biscuit. In fact he didn't even seem to want his tea, as he placed his cup and saucer back on the table. He was sat on the edge of the settee in a way that suggested he wasn't planning to stay long.

Then, as if June sensed Adam's discomfort, she said, "I know it all seems a bit daunting now, but everyone feels the same when they first arrive. Once you settle in, you'll be feeling so much better. We've got a good bunch in here at the moment."

Adam tried to force a smile, but I knew June's words were of little comfort.

"I'm a bit worried that Adam's beginning to shake," I said. "He's had seizures before when he's started to withdraw."

June swiftly switched her gaze to Adam before replying. "Don't worry," she reassured him, "we will be getting a doctor to see you soon and he'll prescribe you some medication which will help with the withdrawal." I glanced at Adam and he was nodding. "If you've finished your tea, I can show you around now if you like?"

We both stood up and followed June as she commenced a tour around the cottage. This is, as you see, where we all eat," she said, gesturing towards the large dining table. "And this is the kitchen." We followed her into another room off of the dining area. It was a fairly large functional looking kitchen. "You will all take turns preparing the meals. We use only fresh foods, as we take nutrition very seriously here."

"Adam used to be a good cook, didn't you Adam?" I said.

"Yeah, used to be," said Adam, sullenly.

"We also have a large washing machine and tumble dryer."

"I don't think I'll need them," said Adam. "I was planning to give my clothes to Fay to take home to wash."

"Oh no, you can't do that, Adam," said June. "We expect people to do their own washing here. It's all about taking responsibility, you see."

Adam gave me a look that suggested he didn't intend to do his own washing despite what June had said. Just then, a young man entered the kitchen and headed over to the fridge. He took out a carton of juice and poured himself a glass. "Kyle, I'd like you to meet Adam," said June. "He's new here. Do you think you could look after him for the first few days?"

"Yeah sure," said Kyle, smiling. He looked very young, and very well. Too well really. It was hard to believe he had any kind of addiction problem.

We then followed June up to the bedrooms, passing another young man on the stairs. "This will be your room," she said. The room was pleasant enough. It contained one single bed with a bedside cupboard, a chest of drawers and a wardrobe.

"There's a lovely view from the window," I said, looking out. But Adam seemed disinterested.

"There's a toilet and a bathroom with a shower just down the hall," said June. "And if we go back downstairs, I'll show you the garden."

June led us out the back door of the cottage into a large garden which boasted an array of pretty wild flowers, a vegetable patch and several weather-worn benches. "We grow a lot of our own vegetables here," June explained. There were a couple of people sat on one of the benches, smoking. A pretty young girl with long blonde hair and a slim dark-haired man, around the same age, wearing a black t-shirt and bleached ripped jeans. I realised that so far, Adam was probably the oldest patient here, by a long chalk.

"It's lovely," I remarked. I was now squinting in the sunlight. It was certainly a beautiful day.

"We have permission to cross the fields to the woods over there," said June, pointing to a line of trees along the horizon. "You'll get the opportunity to go for walks there, when you're feeling fitter."

"When can I visit?" I asked.

"We tend to discourage visitors during the week. We have a strict programme so residents are usually very busy anyway. Weekends are fine."

"That suits me," I said. "It's a long drive from where we live and I work Monday to Friday, so I can only really visit at weekends anyway."

Just then, a smart young woman who I assumed was one of the other therapists, joined us in the garden. "June, the doctor has just arrived."

"Oh good," said June. "We'll get him to check you over, Adam, and then he can prescribe you some medication."

"It's time I got going anyway," I said.

Adam was looking at me now with panic in his eyes. "Let me go with you," he pleaded, clutching my hand. "I've changed my mind. I don't want to stay here now."

"Please don't do this," I said, placing my other hand on his shoulder. "If you want us to have any future together, you have to stay." My tone was deliberately firm, and I was distinctly aware of June watching me. Adam continued to gaze almost longingly into my eyes, and then quite unexpectedly, released my hand.

"Okay," he sighed, turning his face away.

As I began to walk away, June placed a reassuring hand on my arm. "That's good," she said, lowering her voice. "You need to stay strong." I smiled at her, appreciatively. "Now if I was you, I'd just go. Don't drag it out any longer."

Five minutes later I was pulling out of the driveway, after setting my satnav for the long journey home. I turned up the radio and tapped the steering wheel in time to the beat of the music. I felt good. For the first time in a long time, I felt optimistic.

CHAPTER THIRTY-EIGHT

It was Saturday, and Jayne and I were having lunch in town. "So,,. how's Adam doing?" she asked.

"Fine, I think. I feel really hopeful this time."

"I'm really pleased for him," said Jayne, smiling.

"Thank you," I smiled back.

"And what about you? How are *you* doing?"

"Oh, I'm okay," I replied. "I think Adam being away from home for a while has helped." Jayne looked at me questioningly. "What I mean is," I began to explain, "it got to the point when I think I really needed some space, you know?" Jayne nodded, indicating she understood totally.

Suddenly I felt my phone vibrating in my pocket. I took it out just as it was beginning to ring: the familiar sound of Poalo Nutini's *New Shoes.* I glanced at the screen. "Sorry, I better take this," I said. "Hi, Adam!"

"Hi, Fay." Adam sounded better, more like his old self. "Do you think you could come and pick me up?"

"Pick you up?" I looked at Jayne who looked both concerned and baffled at the same time. I looked away again before lowering my voice. "You're supposed to be there for another week."

"I know, but I've had enough," said Adam, in a slightly hushed tone, indicating he didn't wish to be overheard. I was silent for a moment. I was looking down at the table now. This wasn't what I wanted to hear. "Fay? Are you still there?"

I sighed heavily. "Okay," I replied, against my better judgement, "but I don't think I can pick you up today. Can you wait until tomorrow?"

"Tomorrow's fine," said Adam. "What time can I expect you?"

"Oh I don't know," I said. Probably about mid-day."

"That'll be great," said Adam. "I'll look forward to seeing you then."

I hung up. There was a momentary but awkward silence. "You're not really going to pick him up, are you?" asked Jayne, incredulously.

I looked up at Jayne now. "If I don't, he'll find his own way home anyway. At least this way I can make sure he doesn't end up in any pubs along the way." I could tell Jayne was disappointed, particularly with me. I was disappointed with myself. "Besides," I added, "hopefully I'll be able to talk him out of it when I get there."

∞

I arrived at Green Acres around one thirty in the afternoon the following day. Adam was already waiting outside with his bags. I wondered just how long he had been waiting there. There was no talking him out of it either. His mind was made up. I drove in silence for the first ten miles or so. "So, what happened?" I asked, staring straight ahead at the road before me.

"I think one of the therapists had it in for me."

"That just sounds like paranoia to me," I said.

"No, it's not."

"Okay, indulge me. Explain to me why you think one of the therapists had it in for you? What did they do?"

"Well every time we had one of those so called group sessions," began Adam, "he would single me out, just to humiliate me."

"I can't imagine that."

"I'm not lying," exclaimed Adam, defensively.

"I'm not inferring that you are," I said. "What I meant was, I'm sure he wasn't deliberately trying to humiliate you. He was probably just challenging you. It's part of the therapy."

"Well how come I was the only one he focussed on?"

"Perhaps it just felt like that. I can't imagine....."

"Well, you weren't there," interrupted Adam. His tone was now morose.

"Okay, let's not talk about it anymore," I suggested. "You're just lucky I was able to pick you up. I would normally be at work."

"How come you're not?"

"I booked a few days off. Just felt like a needed some time to unwind. I didn't expect this...."

"I'm sorry, but I couldn't have stayed there another day."

I turned on the radio and we sat for a while, not speaking. I glanced sideways at Adam to find he had fallen asleep, his head nodding about with each manoeuvre of the car. I tried to relax and enjoy the drive. One thing I usually didn't mind was driving. I actually found it quite relaxing, providing I wasn't stuck in traffic. But I couldn't relax. In fact the longer I drove, the more tense I became. I tried to banish every negative thought from my mind. *Focus on the positive*, I thought. At least Adam still had the counselling sessions. That was already paid for.

Adam didn't wake up until we were almost home. "I need to get petrol," I said, as I pulled into the petrol station. "Do you need anything from the shop?"

"A couple of cans of beer would be nice," he replied. I looked at Adam in horror. He was smiling. "Just a joke!"

"Well it's not really very funny, is it?"

"Lighten up, can't you?" Then an uninvited thought entered my head. *Was this all just one big joke to him?*

Once I filled up, I crossed the forecourt to the shop. I passed the confectionary on my way to the counter, and with little hesitation, picked up a family bar of fruit and nut chocolate. *I shall eat this whole bar myself*, I thought. And I did.

CHAPTER THIRTY-NINE

It was August, the day of James and Christina's wedding. We had decided to take the train to the City where we had booked into a bed and breakfast for the night. We arrived just in time to freshen up before taking a taxi to the venue.

After we made our way up the flight of stone steps, John and Jennifer greeted us in the entrance to the grand Georgian style hall. John introduced us to James's parents, as it was the first time we had met them. Everyone looked immaculately presented, and as usual I wondered if I was wearing the right outfit for the occasion. Adam looked smarter than he usually did, but I could tell from John's expression when we first arrived that he was quite shocked by Adam's appearance, having not seen him for quite a while.

It was a beautiful day, with barely a cloud in the sky, a gentle breeze cooling the warm summer air. The ceremony was held in the large orangery, overlooking the landscaped gardens and spectacular views of the countryside beyond. We watched Christina walk slowly and gracefully down the aisle, arm in arm with John, the proud father, to the haunting sound of Pachelbel's *Canon in D.* Christina wore a long white mermaid style wedding dress, covered with lace and adorned with beading and sequins, which accentuated her perfect slim figure. Her long auburn hair, crowned by a delicate diamante crystal tiara, cascaded in soft curls down her back.

After the customary photos, we followed the party into a large function room where Adam and I were seated at a large round table with six other people, most of whom we had never met before, an impressive floral display in the centre of the table partly obscuring our view of the guests seated opposite us. Nevertheless, I attempted to engage in small talk whilst Adam seemed a little ill at ease. The four-course meal was delicious, washed down by the complimentary wine that was provided. I didn't complain about Adam having one or two drinks. Since rehab, he had convinced me that although he hadn't been able to maintain complete abstinence, he was now able to keep his drinking under control. Looking back, I now realise just how naive I was to think Adam could control his drinking, any more than I could control the weather or the coming of the seasons.

The incessant chatter died down as John stood up to begin the speeches, followed by James. James thanked the guests for attending and for all their lovely gifts. I briefly wondered whether they'd be pleased with ours, as we couldn't afford to spend much. "I want to thank my parents who have always been very supportive," continued James, "and I also want to thank Christina's parents, john and Jennifer for welcoming me so warmly into the family."

Christina gazed lovingly up at James who was stood beside her as he made his speech, full of wit and adoration for his new wife. I felt the tears pricking my eyes and I swallowed hard. They were two young people in love looking forward to a long and happy life together, and I wondered if what fate had in store for them would be all that they hoped for, or would the years to come be filled with pain and regret that one day would extinguish that light that now burnt so brightly in their eyes?

After the meal, the room was cleared in preparation for the evening's entertainment, whilst the guests socialised in the bar or outside on the terrace. A couple of hours later, we were back in the function room where the tables had been re-arranged to make room for people to dance to the live band that was now set up in one corner of the room.

At midnight a dozen Chinese lanterns were lit and sent up into the night sky. As I stood in the cool evening air, watching the lanterns drift slowly out of sight, until all you could see were the faint dots of red light still burning amidst the blackness of the sky, suddenly I felt very alone in the world, despite the fact that Adam was stood right beside me.

Our taxi picked us up shortly afterwards to take us back to the Bed and Breakfast. It had been a long day and I couldn't wait to climb into bed to get some sleep. Adam insisted on getting into the passenger seat next to the driver. That in itself wasn't unusual. At one time Adam would have chatted affably to the driver for almost the entire journey, except on this occasion, Adam merely slept all the way, whilst I sat in awkward silence in the back of the taxi, willing the journey to be over.

I was dreaming when I was startled from my slumber by what I can only describe as a loud bang. I sat bolt upright in bed. All was in darkness and for a moment, I wondered where I was. I then switched on the bedside lamp. Adam wasn't in bed next to me. Suddenly, a loud groan came from the bathroom. I slid out of bed and padded across the carpet to the bathroom, but the door wouldn't open. There was something heavy blocking it. "Adam! Adam! Are you all right?" I called out. Another groan. "Adam, I can't open the door. Are you all right?" I repeated. Adam somehow managed to shift his position so that I was just able to open the door enough to edge my way in.

The best way to describe Adam would be to say that he was sat in a heap on the floor, leaning against the side of the bath, one leg bent under him, the other out straight. "Are you hurt? Do you think you ought to see a doctor?" I suggested.

"No, no, I'll be fine," insisted Adam, "I just want to go back to bed."

"Okay, well you need to get up then," I said, with less concern in my voice than before. Adam seemed to have no obvious injury, so I attempted to help him up from the floor. It was then that I realised he was sitting in a pool of urine. It was also then that I realised just how little strength Adam now had in his body as i found myself taking most of his weight as he tried to scramble to his feet. "I can't help you up like this, you're too heavy," I panted with both exhaustion and exasperation "You need to turn around and pull yourself up by the side of the bath."

Adam followed my instructions and with something of a struggle, eventually managed to stand up. He then began to totter towards the open doorway. "Wait!" I called out. "You need a wash first." I then grabbed Adam's arm, attempting to steer him towards the wash basin.

"I just want to get back into bed," he protested.

"You're not getting back into bed next to me covered in piss!" I inserted the plug and began turning on the taps, whilst trying not to release my grip on Adam's arm. I then squirted some body wash into the water, quickly checking the temperature before proceeding to wash him down with a flannel i had grabbed from the side. Adam clung on to the edge of the basin, allowing me to release my grip. After washing him down, I rubbed him over briskly with a towel. When I and Adam married, I never imagined that one day I'd be having to do something like this.

I guided Adam back into the bedroom, still half-lit by the bedside lamp which cast shadows on the walls. "Where are we?" asked Adam, glancing around the room with something of a bewildered look on his face.

"In the Bed and Breakfast. We went to James and Christina's wedding yesterday, remember?"

Adam nodded his head but I got the feeling that he couldn't remember. I helped Adam back into his side of the bed, before returning to the bathroom to clean up the mess that had been left behind. By the time I got back into bed myself, Adam was snoring loudly.

When we got up for breakfast later that morning, Adam seemed fine and behaved as though nothing had happened. I, on the other hand, felt shattered, as I had barely slept after Adam had disturbed me in the middle of the night. I was so glad we had decided to take the train. I think we sat mostly in silence over breakfast, as I don't remember much of our conversation. Adam didn't each much, his appetite wasn't what it was, although he looked bloated and overweight. I, on the other hand, felt ravenous, albeit slightly nauseas after too much wine the night before followed by too little sleep.

I do remember one thing though. It was as I looked up at Adam from my breakfast when he spoke to me. I don't remember exactly what he said, but I remember the morning sun was streaming through the bay window behind me, illuminating his sallow complexion that now looked so old and haggard. And as I gazed into those cloudy bloodshot eyes, I remember thinking, *you don't look like my Adam anymore. In fact you don't walk, talk or behave like my Adam anymore.* It was then I think that I truly realised I didn't love Adam anymore and I probably hadn't done for a long time.

However, even after realisation dawned, I still couldn't leave him. Something was stopping me and I really can't be sure exactly what. So I think I just decided to resign myself to the situation I had now found myself in, believing that this may be just about as good as it will ever get.

CHAPTER FORTY

Days, weeks, months passed. It was now Christmas Eve. Adam and I were off to visit Ben, Anita and the girls. Things had seemed better for a while, but I realise now that I was just kidding myself. Probably because that's precisely what I wanted to believe, that things *were* better. What I believe now is that Adam had just become a better liar.

"We better get going," I said.

"Well I'm ready," said Adam. "In fact I've been ready for ages."

"Will you help me load the presents into the car?" I asked.

"Sure," said Adam. "What do you want me to carry?"

"If you take the sacks for the girls," I said, "I'll carry the rest."

"My God, how many presents have you got in here?" said Adam, as he lifted the two large Santa sacks.

"I know," I said. "I've probably overdone it again."

As I started the car, I paused momentarily before driving forward. "I hope you haven't been drinking?" It sounded like a warning, despite my effort to make it sound otherwise.

"No," replied Adam, with a heavy sigh. "I said I wouldn't, didn't I?" He sounded indignant, almost angry.

"Okay, okay," I said, trying my best to smooth things over. "I just don't want anything to spoil today, that's all."

"Would you rather I just didn't come?" Adam's tone was still rather brusque.

"No, of course not."

"Well, are you going to stop going on then?"

We both fell silent. I decided it was best not to say anything more. I didn't want to argue. Not today. I was determined we were going to have a good Christmas this year.

We arrived at Ben and Anita's around five o'clock. Anita's parents, David and Margaret were already there. As we entered the house, the girls came running up the hallway towards us, full of excitement. "Granny Fay! Grandad Adam!" they both cried as they hugged our legs, still too small to reach any higher.

"Merry Christmas, darlings," I said fondly, bending down to give them both a hug and a kiss.

"I think Santa's elves have been very busy this year," joked Adam as he carried the sacks through to the sitting room. "I hope you've both been very good. Otherwise, these sacks may be full of coal."

"Yes, yes, we've been very good, honestly!" they both cried in unison, bouncing up and down as though they had springs on the soles of their feet.

"What would you like to drink, Mum?" asked Ben, as we deposited the presents around the large Christmas tree that stood in the corner of their sitting room.

I glanced over at Anita's parents who were sat quietly together on the settee, both with a cup and saucer on the table in front of them.

"I'll just have a coffee, please," I said.

"How about you, Dad?" asked Ben.

"Have you any beer?" asked Adam. I threw him a critical look. "Non-alcoholic, of course," he added.

"Yeah sure, I'll get you a can."

"I'll get your coffee," said Anita, as both she and Ben disappeared into the kitchen.

For one awkward moment Adam and I stood in silence while Anita's parents sat, smiling up at us but not speaking. David and Margaret weren't the best conversationalists in the world.

"So, how are you?" I said.

"Oh fine, thank you," said Margaret. "How are you?"

"Fine," I replied. "We're both fine, thank you. Aren't we, Adam?" I threw him a look to indicate I needed his help, but he said nothing. It wasn't like Adam to be stuck for words.

I breathed a sigh of relief when Jessica called me over to the table where she and Emily were sitting to show me a picture she had been drawing. "It's a picture of Father Christmas in his sleigh. And those are his reindeer. That's Rudolf at the front because he's got a big red nose."

"That's lovely, darling. You're very clever." Then so as not to show favouritism, "you're both very clever girls."

Moments later, Ben returned with Adam's beer. I noticed he had poured it into a glass and I realised that that was for the benefit of Anita's parents. Adam would usually just drink straight out of the can. I'm not saying that Dave and Margaret were snobs. Perhaps just not so down to earth as Adam and I.

Shortly after that, Anita returned with a mug of coffee. "You prefer a mug, don't you?" said Anita, smiling.

"Yeah, a mug's great," I said.

"We're just putting on a small buffet in the kitchen. It's nearly ready."

Approximately an hour and a half later, we had all eaten and were back in the sitting room. David was stood up with Ben and was discussing the merits of cavity wall insulation, Adam and I were sat on the settee with Margaret, the girls were both sat together on the large armchair opposite us reading a book, and Anita was perched on the pouf. To say Adam was sat down was not entirely accurate. He was in fact lying down on his side with a cushion under his head, still with his feet on the floor. And was beginning to snore. It was obvious that everyone was trying to pretend they hadn't noticed. I continued chatting whilst inside I was a bubbling cauldron of embarrassment and anger.

Suddenly Emily jumped off of the chair and headed towards Adam. She placed both of her tiny hands on Adam and shook him gently. "Wake up, Grandad! You're snoring." As there was no response, she shook him again, a little more vigorously.

Then it happened. So quickly no one could have seen it coming. Still with his eyes closed and with a gruff "fuck off!" Adam lashed out with his free arm, hitting Emily and knocking her backwards off her feet. She landed on her bottom and for a second was totally quiet, stunned it seemed. Then came the wailing and the tears. Without hesitation, Anita was on her feet. She scooped up Emily, hugging her close.

Everyone then threw black looks at me, as though it was all my fault. I turned to Adam. "Wake up!" I shouted, shaking him as hard as I could.

"Err...what? What's going on?" he groaned.

I stared pleadingly at Ben. "Do you want me to help you get him up and get him into the car?" he asked. Apparently, it was time for us to go.

"Yes please, Ben."

As we struggled to get Adam to his feet, Ben taking most of the weight, I kept apologising over and over again. "I'm so sorry everyone. I'm so sorry."

Finally we managed to get Adam to the car and into the passenger seat. "Are you going to be able to get him out the car and into the house at the other end?" asked Ben.

"Well if I can't, he'll just have to stay in the car," I said. "It'll serve him right if he freezes to death."

Just as I was giving Ben a hug good-bye, Anita came outside, still holding Emily, Jessica trotting behind them. Fortunately Emily had stopped crying and there wasn't any obvious injury. Anita was trying to explain to her that it was an accident and that Granddad Adam didn't mean to hit her that he was just dreaming. I gave Anita and the girls a kiss. "Would you mind saying goodbye to David and Margaret for me," I asked. I didn't fancy going back inside to face their disdainful looks.

"Yeah, don't worry I will," said Anita. Hope everything's okay when you get home. Give us a ring when you get back to let us know you're okay."

"Will do. You go back inside. It's cold." I got into the driver's seat. "Bye! Love you!" Then I shut the door and drove off.

I couldn't understand why Adam had managed to get so drunk. I assumed he must have had a drink before we left for Ben and Anita's, despite his promise not to. Even so, he had only been drinking non-alcoholic beer while we were at their house. It wasn't until I finally managed to bring Adam round enough to get him into the house that I discovered his secret. As I helped him take off the jacket he'd been wearing all the time, and then proceeded to hang it up, I heard a chink, the sound of glass against the metal of the coat stand. I felt inside the pockets. In the inside pocket of the jacket was half a bottle of brandy, almost empty.

I think it was then that I decided that this would be the last Christmas we would ever spend together.

CHAPTER FORTY-ONE

It was the third of January. I met Jayne in the usual place outside the café where we almost always ate. They knew us well, we'd been going there for so long. "I think I'm going to have a breakfast," I said. "I'm famished."

"Ooh, I quite fancy that too!" said Jayne. So we both ordered breakfasts, mine with coffee, Jayne's with tea. "I've got loads to tell you," said Jayne, leaning forward on her arms which were folded on the table. I then patiently listened to all of the latest events in her life, when really all I wanted to do was off load my own problems.

Finally our breakfasts arrived which seemed to cause a break in Jayne's train of thought as well as in her conversation, as when she resumed, she said, "so how about you? How are things going with you and Adam?"

Jayne knew about most of the problems Adam and I had been having and had urged me to strongly consider leaving him on more than one occasion. "I've decided," I said, resolutely, "I'm definitely going to leave him as soon as I find a flat."

Jayne's eyes widened. She then reached across the table to place her hand on mine, and with the gentlest of voices, said "you're doing the right thing."

"I know, I said, "but it's still hard."

"It's bound to be," said Jayne, sympathetically. "You've been together for so long. But it's not as though you haven't tried." I nodded in agreement. "Does Ben know yet?"

"No. Adam doesn't even know yet. In fact, I don't know how I'm going to go about it. If I move out while he's there, I know he'll try to stop me."

"Do you think you could move out while he's at work?"

"Yeah, I might have to," I said. "It might sound silly, but it's all the little things that are really beginning to worry me, like what am I going to do with Susie if I can't take her with me? I can't leave her with Adam because I wouldn't trust him to look after her properly."

"Would Ben take her?" suggested Jayne.

“I don’t think so,” I said. “Emily’s a bit scared of dogs ever since their neighbour’s dog jumped over the fence and chased her round the garden. I have to shut Susie outside now, or in another room, whenever they visit.”

“Well, I’ll ask around if you like. I’d take her but I don’t think it would be fair on the cats.” Jayne had two cats. They were brother and sister and named Mickey and Minnie, no doubt due to their matching black and white coats.

“No of course not,” I said. “If I can’t find a home for Susie, I’ll just have to see if the Dogs Trust will take her.”

∞

When I took Susie out for a walk that evening, I felt she knew something had changed. As she trotted alongside me, occasionally she would look up at me, and in her eyes I could see a sense of abandonment. If she could speak, I was certain she would say, “please don’t give me up, because you’re my mum and I love you.” I felt so guilty, almost like I was planning to give up a child. However at the same time, I knew I was just being ridiculous. Susie would probably be far less upset about it all than I would be.

It was a clear night so I decided to take the long route back home. I needed time to think. Then I spotted it. A large piece of white card in the window of one of the new flats that had been built just a few streets away from our house. The card read: *2 bedroom flat to let. Telephone: 07769265728.*

I had my mobile phone on me so I telephoned the number on the card straight away. “Hello?” came the voice at the other end of the phone. It was a deep masculine voice.

“Oh, hello,” I began, “I’m ringing up about the ad in the window for the flat to let. Is it still available?”

“Yes, it is. Would you like to view it?”

“Yes, definitely,” I said, and I wondered if I sounded too eager.

“Can you come by tomorrow?” he suggested.

“Tomorrow’s fine.”

“Okay, I’ll meet you outside the flat at eleven o’clock, if that’s okay with you?”

“Yeah, that’s perfect for me,” I said.

"Great. I'll see you then. My name's Jim by the way."

"My name's Fay.

∞

I met Jim outside the flat at eleven the next morning as arranged. He pulled up in his car with whom I assumed was his wife, just as I arrived. They both got out of the car. "Hi, is it Fay?" he asked.

"Yes," I replied and went over to him to shake hands.

"This is Maggie," he said.

"Pleased to meet you," I said, smiling, trying my best to make a good first impression.

I followed Jim and Maggie into the empty flat. The rooms were all of a reasonable size, and as I looked around, I mentally furnished them with my own possessions. The sitting room and bedrooms were carpeted, but the kitchen, bathroom and hallway were covered in laminate wood flooring. There were blinds up at all the windows, and the built-in kitchen cupboards with granite work tops were smart and modern.   It all looked very clean and newly decorated, and very tastefully at that. "This is just perfect," I said.

"We also have a garden out the back," said Maggie. I followed her and Jim to a fairly large patch of lawn running along the small block of flats, with a few small shrubs around its borders.   "We maintain it," explained Maggie, "so you don't need to worry about that."

"Can I put my own garden furniture out here?" I asked, already picturing myself relaxing on a lounger, the sun beating down, with a book and a cool drink in my hand.

"Of course."

"This is exactly what I'm looking for," I said, enthusiastically. "How much is it?"

"Five hundred and twenty a month," replied Jim.

"That's fine," I said. "When will it be available?"

"As soon as you like," said Jim. "Have you got somewhere else you need to give notice to?"

"Not really," I said. "I should be able to move in pretty quickly. Would you need a deposit?"

"Yes it will be a month and a half's rent in advance," said Jim. "The thing is Maggie and I are going away on holiday on Wednesday, so ideally we would like to formalise everything before we go. I can draw up the lease agreement today, so if you are able to pay the deposit tomorrow, you can have the keys right away."

"What about references?" I asked.

"I don't think we need to bother about that," said Jim. "I think I'm a pretty good judge of character."

I couldn't believe how easy it was. It was like it was meant to be. So I agreed to meet Jim again the next day with a cheque, to sign the lease agreement and collect the keys. The only problem was, I wasn't entirely sure that I could afford it.

CHAPTER FORTY-TWO

I was able to start packing some things up pretty much straight away without Adam even noticing. While he was out I'd start emptying cupboards and drawers I knew he never went into. I was surprised to find so much rubbish we had accumulated. Bank statements more than ten years old, product manuals for things we no longer owned, dead batteries, broken toys and empty shoe boxes. A lot of stuff either went to the charity shop or to the tip.

It was whilst I was emptying one of the cupboards that I found it, something I had almost forgotten that I had: a large shoe box, covered with pretty floral wrapping paper, now faded by time. I carefully removed the lid and inside, sure enough, there they still were, precious moments from the past preserved for more than a quarter of a century. There was a pair of Ben's booties and one of his first sleep suits, pure white, embellished with a yellow giraffe. They both looked so small. There was a bundle of greeting cards, tied together with blue ribbon, congratulating Adam and I on the birth of our baby boy. And there was a small photo album. As I opened it, the first photograph I saw was one of Adam, Ben and I. I was holding Ben who was so small; the photo must have been taken only shortly after he was born. We were standing in front of the fireplace, Adam's arm around me. I could just spy the head of the black Murano glass cat on the mantelpiece behind us, and next to that stood a miniature yellow rose bush in a pretty blue and yellow ceramic planter. Adam and I were both smiling with pride and joy. Our smiles were genuine, not false or forced, there's no doubt about that. I tried to recall who had taken the photo. Who was holding the camera. Then I remembered.............

The telephone rang. I was holding Ben so Adam got up and picked up the receiver. "Hello." There was a pause and then Adam said, "Thank you. But Fay did all the work." I stared at Adam with a quizzical look. "Yes, we called him Ben." It was obvious now. Someone was congratulating Adam on the arrival of our first child. "Yes, she's here. I'll just get her." I then stood up with Ben still in my arms. "It's Jayne," said Adam, handing me the receiver. As I took the receiver, I passed Ben to Adam.

"Hi, Jayne!" I said, cheerfully. "You're back from holiday then? Did you have a nice time?"

"Yeah, I did, thanks. I had a lovely time," Jayne replied. "But I thought you were going to wait until I got back to give birth."

"I tried to," I laughed, "but unfortunately Ben had other ideas."

"When can I come round?" asked Jayne. "I'm dying to see him."

"How about tomorrow?"

"Yeah, that's good for me. What time?"

"Any time in the afternoon. I'm usually a bit disorganised in the morning, I'm afraid."

The following day Jayne turned up around three in the afternoon. Ben was asleep in his carry cot on the floor in the sitting room. "Oh my God, he's gorgeous!" she cried, gazing down at Ben. "Was it really painful?" Trust Jayne to ask that.

"To be honest, yes it was," I said. A look of horror flashed across Jayne's face "But, it all seems well worth it now." I cast a smile over Ben, as he still lay sleeping.

"I've got him a present," said Jayne, eagerly, handing me a small blue gift bag.

I opened the bag. Inside was a pair of white booties tied up with blue ribbon and a small wind-up musical carousel. "It's lovely," I said, giving Jayne a kiss on the cheek. "I also got you this," said Jayne, producing the miniature yellow rose bush in its ceramic planter, which I proceeded to place on the mantelpiece beside the black Murano glass cat.

Then Ben began to stir and grizzle. "Is he waking up?" asked Jayne, excitedly.

"Yes," I said. "He may be due another feed." I picked up Ben as he started to open his eyes. "Look who it is," I said, tenderly. "It's Auntie Jayne. And she's brought you a present."

"Aah," cooed Jayne. "I've got my camera. Let me take a photo of you three together."

"Okay," I said. "Adam!" Adam appeared in the doorway to the kitchen. "Jayne wants to take a photo of us with Ben."

"Okay." Adam walked over and stood beside me in front of the fireplace, putting his arm around my waist, as I cradled Ben in my arms.

Jayne clicked the shutter. "That's lovely," she said, smiling. "I'll get a copy for you as well."

CHAPTER FORTY-THREE

Although I intended not to tell Adam, to move out the furniture when he was at work and just leave a note, in the end I just couldn't do it. So one night I told him.

"Have you got someone else?" he asked.

"No," I replied.

"Then why do you want to leave?"

"That's typical of you," I said, exasperated. "You assume that the only reason I would want to leave is because of someone else. Even now you're still in denial. You still won't accept responsibility for your behaviour."

"What can I do to change your mind?"

I just shook my head.

"Is it the drinking?"

"You know it is."

"If I stop drinking, will you stay?"

"But you won't stop."

"I will. I promise you I will. As long as you don't go."

"It's too late."

∞

I don't think Adam really believed I was going until the day actually arrived. I was hoping he would be at work but Adam was off sick again, so I suggested he go out. I really didn't want to put him (or myself) through any further unnecessary trauma. When the removal van turned up, I had just finished packing up the boxes. I really wasn't taking that much, leaving much of the furniture and appliances behind for Adam. I didn't want to leave him with nothing. I intended to buy myself new stuff. Dad had very kindly offered to lend me some more money until the house was sold. I agreed to pay him back, once my share of the equity came through, as well as the remaining money I still owed him which he had leant us for Adam's rehab. For some inexplicable reason, Adam's debt to my father had become my debt, and my debt alone.

Adam refused to go out as I suggested, so when the removal men began loading the van with my stuff, Adam begged me to reconsider, stating he never thought I'd really go through with it. He began crying and pleading with me. "I'll change. I promise you, I'll change. Please, don't go!"

"Please, Adam, you're just making this so much harder. I don't want to hurt you....."

"Then why are you doing this? You know I can't live without you." Adam was sobbing now.

Tears welled up in my eyes as I felt my heart being ripped out. "Well Adam, I can't live with you, not anymore. It's killing me."

"Please, mate," said Adam to one of the removal men, his eyes still wet with tears, "just hold on a minute." Adam positioned himself between the removal man and the door, in an attempt to impede his progress. Without uttering a single word, the removal man looked at me, his expression suggesting he didn't quite know how to handle this situation he had found himself in.

"Will you just give us a minute?" I asked the removal man. "Please?"

The removal man nodded, carefully placed the large box he was carrying back on the floor, and then went outside.

"Adam, please just sit down for a minute, will you?" Adam did as I asked. I sat down next to him on the settee, then turning to face him, I placed my hands in his. I took a deep breath in an attempt to slow down my breathing, so that my tone of voice was now calm yet deliberate. "Adam, I am leaving, you've just got to accept that. You have chosen the life you want. But it's not the life I want, not anymore."

"The life I want is with you. Haven't I proved that over the years? There's never been anyone else but you. I've never been unfaithful to you, not once."

"I know, and I believe you. But to be honest, I would have preferred that," I said. "I would have preferred it if you had been unfaithful."

"I don't understand. What are you saying?"

"What I'm saying is what you've been doing is worse, far worse."

"What can be worse than that?" asked Adam,

"Watching someone you love slowly destroying themselves in front of your very eyes, and you can't do a blind thing about it. That's worse."

"So you *do* still love me," said Adam, smiling.

"I still love the man I married, but not the person you've become." My voice started to shake now as I tried to hold back the tide of tears that swelled within me.

"But I'm still the same person."

I just shook my head. I then swallowed hard and tried to compose myself before speaking again. "Look, Adam. I don't want to part on bad terms. If you really make an effort to deal with your drinking, if that's what you want, then maybe, just maybe we still may have some kind of future together. But today, !'m afraid, I'm still leaving."

CHAPTER FORTY-FOUR

I knew Adam would react to me leaving him in one of two ways. He would either be compelled to re-evaluate his life and the choices he had made, realising that he now needed to take control of his life and his drinking. Or he would simply give up altogether and basically start to drink himself to death. Unfortunately, but not surprisingly, he chose the latter, whilst ensuring I still remained bound to him by guilt, pity, or some misguided sense of obligation.....I couldn't say what it was exactly because even I didn't really know for sure.

Adam eventually lost his job due to the fact that he was never there. He finally agreed to sell the house, and I helped him get his name down on the council housing list as no private landlord was going to take on a tenant who was an out of work drunk, at least not without a guarantor. I also helped Adam apply for benefits, although it seemed as though each time I completed and returned one form, they would just send me out another. Because Adam had no income now, and we had no remaining credit available, I knew that unless I sold the house soon, we were in danger of losing everything as I could no longer afford the mortgage repayments on my own. The thing was I couldn't show any potential buyers around the house because Adam would either be unconscious and languishing in bed, or slumped on the sofa in his underwear pissed out of his head and talking total gibberish.

Adam's GP referred him to the Substance Misuse team. He was put on the waiting list for NHS funded detox and rehab, although we were told it would probably be months before a bed became available for him, if at all. Meanwhile he was assigned an alcohol counsellor, Bernice, although he rarely turned up to see her. Some-how he did manage to stagger round to the off licence every day however which was conveniently situated around the corner from our house. Adam stopped washing and shaving, losing all pride in his appearance. He also stopped eating, despite any encouragement from me. Before my very eyes, Adam was fading away.

I hadn't seen Adam for three or four days. The last time I had spoken to him was more than twenty four hours ago. He said he needed to see me and he sounded desperate, but I had barely managed to muster up the energy to get out of bed myself. As I opened the front door to the house, I wondered, would this be the day I find him dead in his bed or at the foot of the stairs with his neck broken?

"Adam!" I called from the hallway.

"I'm in here," came Adam's reply. I followed his voice, finding him sat on the settee in the sitting room, just wearing a pair of boxer shorts and a t-shirt. The television wasn't on. He seemed to just be sat there in silence staring into space. His body was covered in scratches, cuts and bruises, no doubt from all the falls he was having. His legs were spindly, almost bowed, the muscles starting to waste away. His grey hair stuck out at all angles in long clumps, having not been washed for I don't know how long. A growth of grey bristly whiskers covered his chin. The lower lids of his eyes were bright red like a blood hound's. He looked and smelled like a tramp.

"When was the last time you ate?" I asked.

"I dunno....about 3 days ago, I think." There was in fact no evidence that he had prepared himself anything to eat since I had seen him last. How long could he live without food altogether? I stared at him, incredulously. It was hard to believe that I once allowed him to make love to me. Now I could barely look at him.

"Why are you doing this to yourself?" I asked.

"I don't know."

"It makes no sense."

"I know."

"Please, just tell me, what are you getting out of it?"

"I don't know," said Adam, sullenly, his head lowered with his arms resting on his knees.

"Please, I want to understand," I said, almost pleadingly, "what exactly do you get out of it?"

"Pleasure?" Adam replied, although the inflection in his voice indicated he was answering my question with another question.

"Really?" I asked, in disbelief. "How is that possible? You spend most of your time alone drinking until you lose consciousness. You've no friends, or at least none that you see anymore. You look miserable. You can't possibly feel well."

"I don't," said Adam, his head still lowered. "I feel terrible."

"Look, do you think you could eat something?" I suggested.

"I'm not hungry."

"Don't you realise that if you carry on like this, you're going to die?"

"Yeah, you're probably right," said Adam, resignedly.

"So why, Adam, why?"

"Because I have no reason not to."

"But you have. You have a son. You have Granddaughters."

"But I haven't got you anymore, have I?"

"No. But we might still have had a chance. When I left, you said you wanted to win me back. Don't you see, all this is doing is driving me further away?"

"I need to go back to bed," said Adam, as though he hadn't even heard the last thing that I said. With that, he stood up and made his way back upstairs, without so much as making eye contact with me.

CHAPTER FORTY-FIVE

The next day I decided to telephone Bernice and speak to her myself. "Hi, Bernice?"

"Yes, speaking."

"This is Fay Reynold's. Adam's wife."

"Oh, hi, Fay. What can I do for you?"

"I don't know. I mean, I'm not sure what you *can* do. I just want some advice I suppose. I know Adam hasn't been coming to his appointments. I've been reminding him....you see he just forgets everything these days.....but even when I remind him.......short of dragging him there myself....."

"Really the only way I can help him is if he wants to help himself," said Bernice.

"What do you suggest I do, then?" I asked. "Should I move back in with him to keep a closer eye on him?"

"Is that what you want?"

"No. But I feel guilty standing by, just watching him slowly kill himself."

"I understand how difficult this must be for you, but it's not your responsibility."

"Then whose is it?" My question was met with silence, so I went on. "If I was sure he had a choice..."

"He does have a choice," said Bernice.

"Does he? I wish I could be sure of that."

"I get the impression," began Bernice, "that you are in desperate need of support yourself. We offer counselling for families and carers as well. Would you like me to refer you? I think you would find it really helpful."

I considered it for a moment. "Yes, please, maybe it would help."

"Ok, I'll do that straight away then, Fay. You'll probably get a phone call in a couple of days. Meanwhile, please remember, Adam's behaviour is not your responsibility, it's his. And please do not feel guilty about putting yourself first for once."

"Thank you."

∞

It was my second session with my counsellor, Andrea. I wasn't entirely sure how much it was helping, but she was the first person I felt I could be completely honest with. Neither Dad, Ben nor even Jayne really knew how I truly felt, what dark thoughts I was harbouring.

"I call in every evening on my way home from work," I said, looking through the open window before me, vaguely noticing a beautiful yellow rose bush growing against a low wall outside. "Just to check on him, check he's still alive." I took a deep breath. "As I open the front door, part of me is dreading what I might find, but part of me is almost hoping that what I might find will mean it's all over, once and for all." I turn my head to meet Andrea's gaze, her face blurred by the tears that now filled my eyes. "Have you any idea how that feels? To realise that you hope to find the man you once loved dead? The man you once thought you could never live without, the man who is the father of your only child."

"I understand this is extremely difficult for you at present," said Andrea. "That you are feeling very confused by your feelings." Andrea's voice was gentle, almost soothing. "Is it important to you to call in to see him every day?"

I thought for a moment. "I don't know," I said. "I think it must be. Although I'd rather just never have to see him again. I'd rather not hear from him again. But then I'd still probably worry anyway, wonder if he's okay."

"What you seem to be saying," said Andrea, "is that you do still worry about him, that you do still care, despite what you've said about sometimes hoping to find him...." Andrea hesitated in order to choose her words carefully....."gone."

"I suppose."

"When we lose someone or something, we can experience many different emotions, sometimes conflicting emotions," said Andrea.

"I do feel that I've lost someone," I said. "But I feel I lost him a long time ago. What's left is just a shell of his former self."

"So what you're saying is you feel you have already lost the man you married, the man you fell in love with, and it's this loss you are mourning? The person you wish were gone now, isn't him?"

"No, it isn't."

"So what you may be saying is, what you sometimes wish were over is not his life, but the addiction?"

When she said it like that, it didn't sound so bad, but it didn't seem to stop me from still experiencing an incredible sensation of guilt.

"I used to have this dream," I said. "One of those recurring dreams." I gazed out of the window again at the yellow rose bush. "I would dream that I had lost Adam. Sometimes in the dream he would leave me for another woman. Sometimes in the dream he would die. When I woke up, the feeling was always the same, an awful empty feeling inside, just for the first few seconds. Then I'd realise it was just a dream, a nightmare really. And I'd feel such a sense of relief. I never thought I'd lose him like this...."

"Is that how you feel now, that empty feeling inside?"

"Yes, I think it is. But it's now a nightmare I can't wake up from."

Andrea said nothing, but I could feel her eyes on me. Then I carried on, almost as though she had asked me to, but without speaking. "Sometimes at night when I'm all alone in my flat and everything is silent, like the whole world is asleep apart from me, I have a sudden feeling of fear, of panic, of dread really. And it's like I'm in the middle of a nightmare but I'm awake, or at least I think I'm awake. It's like when you dream you've woken up but really you're still asleep. Do you ever have dreams like that?"

"Yes, I think I have," said Andrea. "Do you sometimes wish your life were a dream now that you could wake up from?"

"Yes, I think I wish the last twenty-five years had been a dream."

"As long as that? Why twenty-five years?"

"Because that was when Ben was a baby. That was when I remember feeling the happiest I have ever felt." There was no denying it, we did have some happy times after that. Many probably. But none could compare with how perfectly happy I felt then, when the two of us made three, our beautiful little family.

I continued to gaze through the window at the yellow rose bush, and wondered if its simple beauty and perfection could be a symbol of hope in a world that otherwise now looked so grey and ugly.

CHAPTER FORTY-SIX

It was nine o'clock on a Sunday morning. I was just enjoying my lie in when I heard a knock at the door. I chose to ignore it. Then there was another knock, louder this time. They sounded persistent. *Perhaps I better see who it is*, I thought.

I threw back the duvet and slid out of bed. I then quickly put on my dressing gown and headed up the hallway towards the front door. I could see the shape of a person through the glass, but could not make out who it was. I opened the door to find a woman standing before me that I did not recognise. "Is it Fay?"

"Yes."

"It's your husband, Adam. I think he collapsed at the bottom of Sycamore drive. The ambulance is with him now. He's asking for you. He knew your address but couldn't remember your telephone number."

"Thanks," I said. "I'll just get dressed."

As I was driving there I wondered, *what was Adam doing out walking at that time on a Sunday morning*? Then I remembered. The off licence was situated at the bottom of Sycamore Drive and that opened at eight.

By the time I arrived there, there wasn't an ambulance in sight. I returned to my flat. There was no point in me driving over to the hospital yet as I wasn't sure which hospital they would have taken him to. So I put the kettle on and made myself a much needed cup of tea. I waited approximately another ten minutes before ringing the Accident and Emergency department at the nearest hospital. "I believe the ambulance may have brought my husband to you," I explained.

"What's his name?" the woman at the other end of the phone asked.

"It's Adam Reynolds."

"Yes, he's here."

"Is there a doctor or a nurse I can speak to about him?" I asked.

"Just a moment....I'll see."

I waited so long at the end of the phone, I started to wonder if I'd been forgotten. Then suddenly I was almost startled by a different and louder voice in my ear. "Hello, Staff Nurse Roberts, can I help you?"

"Oh, hello, I just wanted to speak to someone about my husband, Adam Reynolds," I began hurriedly. "I've been very concerned about him. He's constantly falling and is eating very little. I know he's been asking to go into rehab, and we are trying to arrange this, although a bed may not be available until January. He really needs help now. Do you think you'll be keeping him in?"

"Well I'm not sure yet whether we'll be keeping him in or sending him home as he hasn't seen the doctor yet. But he'll most probably be sent back home."

I sighed. "The thing is, Adam and I are separated, so you see he's all alone at home, and very vulnerable."

Nurse Roberts was silent for a moment. "I understand, Mrs Reynolds, but we'll know more when the doctor sees him."

"Okay," I replied, with an even deeper sigh, resigned to the fact that there was nothing more I could do at this point. "If you need to speak to me can you ring me please? I'll give you my mobile number."

"Yes, that's fine."

I reeled off my mobile number.

"Okay, we'll ring you when we have some more information."

"Thank you."

∞

There was no point in me driving over to the hospital just yet. Besides, I'd spent too many hours already waiting around in A & E departments; hours I would never get back. I didn't believe in God but I prayed they would keep him in. What else did he need to do before someone would help him?

More than an hour had passed by before I received a phone call from the hospital. "Is that Mrs Reynolds?"

"Yes."

"Your husband's ready to be discharged. Do you think you could come and pick him up?"

"You're not keeping him in then?"

"No. He can go home."

"Okay," I sighed. "I'll leave in a couple of minutes."

"Do you know how long you'll be?"

"About half an hour, I should think."

"That's great. Thank you."

When I arrived at the hospital, I parked outside the Accident and Emergency department. As I entered the building, I walked past rows of people sat waiting to be seen. I scanned their faces but could not see Adam, so I turned into the corridor that led into another waiting area, where I found Adam sitting talking to a fellow patient, seemingly without a care in the world. "Oh hello, Fay," said Adam, attempting to stand up. Without saying a word, I slid my hand under his upper arm to help him up. "It was nice talking to you," was his parting words to the stranger.

"You too."

I walked on ahead, whilst Adam trailed behind. "Have you got any change?" he asked, as we walked past a drinks vending machine. "I'm really parched."

"You'll have to wait until we get home," I snapped, without breaking my stride. As I exited the department and headed towards the car, I felt a slight pang of guilt. I *did* have change. I *could* have bought him a drink.

As I pulled out of the car park, I opened the window. "God, you stink!" I exclaimed.

"What of?"

"I don't know. You just stink. And you look like a tramp." I realised just how cruel and disparaging my words were almost as soon as I uttered them.

"I must admit," said Adam, rubbing his chin, "I do need a shower and a shave."

When we arrived back at the house, the first thing Adam did was go into the kitchen and crack open a can of beer. At least it wasn't the super strength stuff, but I wondered if there was any of that left hidden around the house. Adam sat down on the settee. After a few mouthfuls of beer, I said "go upstairs now and have a shower."

"In a minute."

"No, go now, while I'm here, in case you fall."

"Okay," he acquiesced. With something of a struggle, Adam got up from the settee and made his way upstairs. Whilst he was having his shower, I began to search the house for his secret hoard of alcohol. I looked in all his usual hiding places. He was really that predictable. I only found one can, one can of super strength beer, 9% to be exact. I stared at the black can, imprinted with gold coloured writing. In block capitals I read the words: *please drink responsibly*. I scoffed. *Please drink responsibly. Like that's gonna work! Not putting 9% beer on the shelves, that would be the responsible thing to do.*

I snapped back the ring pull and poured the can of beer down the sink. I checked the fridge. Adam only had one more can of beer left, that is, normal strength beer, 4.5% to be exact. *He'll need some more*, I told myself.

By the time Adam came back down stairs, he looked and smelled a lot better. He'd also washed his hair and shaved, and was wearing clean clothes. "You look much better," I said. "Can I get you something to eat?"

"I don't feel hungry."

"Have something. Even if it's just soup. You can't keep drinking on an empty stomach."

Adam sighed. "Okay, I'll have some soup."

CHAPTER FORTY-SEVEN

It was just five days later when it happened. I wasn't entirely surprised as it was one of those things I feared would happen all along. Nevertheless, it was still a shock. I drove home from work as usual, debating in my mind whether or not to call in on Adam along the way. I had spoken to him about three hours earlier when he rang me on my mobile, asking me if he would be seeing me later. It was obvious he had been drinking then as his speech was slurred, so I half expected to find him asleep or unconscious as was often the case.

I pulled up onto the drive, noticing the curtains were still closed in the sitting room and in the bedroom. He rarely bothered opening the curtains now. I inserted the key in the lock. As I pushed open the door, the first thing I noticed was splashes of red on the floor and on a pair of Adam's shoes that had been discarded in the hallway. Then I saw a body lying at the foot of the stairs. And it didn't seem to be moving. As I cautiously stepped through the doorway and entered the hall, I realised the body was Adam. The splashes of red were blood. As I got closer, I saw his face. For a split second I thought he must be dead. But he wasn't. He was alive and conscious, struggling to lift his head from the floor.

"What the hell have you done?" I exclaimed.

"I don't know," said Adam.

"Did you fall down the stairs?"

"No I don't think so," he replied. Then I noticed one of the pictures on the wall above the stairs had fallen off and smashed.

"I think you did," I said. "How long have you been here?"

"I don't know. My neck really hurts," Adam groaned, trying to lift his head again. "Will you help me to get up?"

"No, don't move!" At least I was cool-headed enough to realise that Adam shouldn't be moved if he had a neck injury. "I'm going to ring for an ambulance."

"No, don't," complained Adam. "I don't want to go to hospital."

"Don't be ridiculous," I berated. "You've fallen down stairs, there's blood everywhere, and you could have a broken neck."

Eventually the ambulance arrived. The paramedics told me I had done the right thing, not attempting to move Adam. With some difficulty they managed to fix a brace to his neck and manoeuvre him onto a backboard before carrying him out of the house and into the ambulance. I threw a few things of Adam's together in a bag and followed the ambulance to the hospital.

∞

"Because your neck is quite short, it was difficult to get a clear picture of the base of your neck, but it looks as though you may have a fracture," explained the doctor. "What we need to do now is take you for a scan."

"What, now?" Adam asked.

"Yes, now."

As they wheeled Adam away on the trolley, the doctor nodded to me, saying, "you can wait here." So I sat down on the hard plastic chair and waited. I then realised that my throat was extremely dry. What I would have done for a drink. When they returned, the doctor said, "I just need to get the Radiologist to look at the scan result." He then went away but returned shortly afterwards, walking straight over to Adam who was still lying on his back on the trolley. Whilst looking down on him, the doctor raised his voice slightly so that Adam could hear between the two orange blocks on each side of his head, and perhaps also to emphasise the importance of what he was telling him. "Adam, it is what we suspected. Your neck is in fact broken. So you mustn't move your head or neck at all. Do you understand?"

"Yes," said Adam. "But the back of my head hurts and my arm's really painful." Adam lifted his left arm.

"The injury to your head is the least of your problems," said the doctor. "And as for your arm, that's most likely referred pain from your neck. We will get you some pain relief soon." The doctor began to walk away, whilst speaking to me in hushed tones. "There are in fact four fractures, quite close to the spinal cord. He's lucky as so far all his limbs are still working, but if he moves his head, even just a fraction, he could end up being quadriplegic. That's the worst case scenario, but I think it's fair that I make you aware of this."

I nodded and surprised myself at how calm I felt. Maybe it was the shock, I thought. I almost felt like a bystander in someone else's dream, someone else's nightmare.

"I'm really uncomfortable," said Adam. "I need to sit up." Adam tried to raise his head.

"You can't!" I exclaimed. "They told you to keep still!"

"But I've got to!" Adam began trying to sit up again, despite his head being weighed down by the blocks on each side of his head.

I laid my hands on his chest, trying to prevent him from moving. "Stop it!" Suddenly I didn't feel calm anymore. "Do you want to be paralysed?"

It seemed an age before the doctor returned, by which time my anxiety levels felt sky high. "He won't keep still," I said, in exasperation. "He keeps trying to sit up."

"You mustn't move," said the doctor, firmly. "We're going to give you some pain relief now and something to make you feel more relaxed."

Thank God, I thought, and found myself saying, "I think he needs something to knock him out."

Just then a nurse came along to insert a needle and cannula into a vein in Adam's arm. Three syringes of liquid were then injected into his arm. Almost immediately, Adam's body seemed to relax and his eyes began to close. He was then attached to a machine by leads monitoring his pulse, respiration, blood pressure and oxygen saturation levels.

"I have spoken to the hospital in Stoke," explained the doctor. "They are willing to take your husband, so as soon as transport is ready, we will send him there. It's the best place as they're specialists in this type of injury."

"Okay," I nodded, already feeling much calmer. I returned to Adam's side and was surprised and relieved to find that he was now actually starting to gently snore. Then suddenly the machine began to emit a loud beeping sound. I gave the nurse who appeared suddenly a questioning look. She placed an oxygen mask over Adam's nose and mouth. "His oxygen levels are just a little low," she explained. "Nothing to worry about." She then left just as swiftly.

The beeping sound had stopped and I breathed a sigh of relief. Realising just how tired I was now beginning to feel, I dragged the plastic chair up beside the trolley and sat down beside Adam. Then waited.

Waiting for an ambulance to take Adam to Stoke seemed like forever. When it eventually arrived, I was asked if I was travelling to Stoke with him. By now it was gone eleven o'clock in the evening and I knew Stoke was probably at least an hour and a half away by car. "I'm not sure," I said, glancing at the nurse who was stood beside me.

"If I was you," she suggested. "I'd go home and get some sleep." The tone of her voice was soft and reassuring. "There's nothing else you can do now. And besides, I understand you are separated, so no one expects any more than what you've done already."

I smiled and let out a sigh of relief. "Thank you," I said, gratefully. "I think I will go home now. I'm very tired."

I went over to Adam just before they wheeled him away on his stretcher. I looked down at his face, still sandwiched between the two orange blocks. "Bye, Adam, I'll see you soon." I squeezed his hand briefly. He smiled up at me, but seemed to be floating off to somewhere else very far away.

∞

It seemed too late to ring anyone by the time I got home, so I decided to wait until the next day. Jayne and I were due to fly out to Tunisia on the Sunday. It was our first holiday together since we had taken Ben and Sarah to Devon when they were only nine and ten. My last holiday abroad was with Adam and that was only four years ago, but predictably he drank too much and therefore it was spoilt. Jayne and I decided to go somewhere neither of us had ever been before, so five months previously we booked a holiday to Tunisia. We had both been counting down the days ever since. I was determined not to let Jayne, or myself down. Although I did feel a little guilty.

The first person I rang the next day was Ben. "Hi, Ben. I'm afraid I've got some bad news about Dad."

"Oh my God, what?" came Ben's concerned voice at the other end of the phone.

"He had a fall downstairs and broke his neck. He's in Stoke hospital." Initially, this news was met with complete silence. In fact, I began to wonder whether Ben and I had been cut off. "Ben? Are you still there?"

Eventually, Ben broke the silence. "Well how bad is it? I mean, is he gonna be paralysed or what?"

"I don't know for sure. Hopefully not. They're hoping to operate today or tomorrow."

"Well I can't say I'm surprised," said Ben. "He's lucky he hasn't already broken his neck before now."

"I know."

"Do you think this will finally make him see sense?" Ben still surprised me at how mature he was now. In fact, I sometimes wondered whatever happened to that small innocent boy I strove so hard to protect from the harshness of reality.

"I hope so," I said. "If this doesn't, I don't know what else will."

"Isn't it tomorrow you're supposed to be going on holiday with Jayne?" asked Ben.

"Yes it is. I don't want to let Jayne down, but I feel a bit guilty about going now with what has happened to your Dad."

"Don't feel guilty, Mom! You deserve this holiday. He's brought all this on himself, after all."

"I know."

"Go and enjoy yourself. There's nothing else you can do now anyway."

"I suppose you're right, Ben."

So then I telephoned Jayne. I gave her the news about Adam but assured her that I would still be going on holiday with her. I was relieved that Ben had given me permission to go and enjoy myself. I don't know what I would have done if he had said he thought I shouldn't go, because I really wanted to go. I wondered, *did that make me a selfish person, a bad person?*

"This might sound a bit selfish," said Jayne, "but I'm really glad you're still coming on holiday. I can't deny I would have been bitterly disappointed if you had said you weren't, but I do really think you deserve this holiday as well."

CHAPTER FORTY-EIGHT

So we were set. We were definitely still going to Tunisia. I telephoned the hospital before I left to see if there was any more news and to let them know I would be out of the country for the following week. I gave them Ben's telephone number although Ben had said that he would also contact the hospital himself. When I phoned, they still hadn't operated because apparently Adam had suffered four seizures which was something of a concern considering his fragile condition. Well there was nothing more I could do now but leave Adam in the hospital's capable hands, so after loading my case and hand luggage into the car and quickly scanning the flat to ensure I hadn't forgotten anything, I left to collect Jayne for our journey to the airport.

∞

Now all those months of anticipation melted away as Jayne and I were at last sunning ourselves beside the hotel pool in Skanes. I reclined my sunbed and leant back, closing my eyes, the sea breeze gently caressing my cheek. I felt wonderfully relaxed. This was just what I needed and the only way to truly escape, by putting miles and miles of land and ocean between me and my problems.

Suddenly, I heard a child's laughter. I turned my head and shielded my eyes from the sun. Despite wearing my sunglasses, the sun was still so bright, with not a cloud in the sky for it to hide behind. I don't think I had ever seen a sky so blue. A little boy, around three years old, wearing nothing but shorts and a Mickey Mouse hat, ran past our sun beds, chasing a large inflatable ball, followed closely by an older boy around ten years old. For a split second I thought, *it's Ben. I'm sure of it*. Then a split second later, I realised that it couldn't possibly be. Ben was all grown up now with children of his own. I felt a tug on my heart. Oh, how I missed those days when Adam, Ben and I were a proper little family.

"Do you fancy a cocktail?" Jayne asked.

I looked at my watch. It was just midday. "Why not?" I replied. "Shall we see what the cocktail of the day is?"

Jayne stood up, wrapped her sarong around her and slipped on her flip flops. I watched as she padded towards the pool-side bar. Then I leant back again against the sunbed and closed my eyes. I don't know how long Jayne had been gone, but I must have drifted off for a minute or two, because she was suddenly back beside me. "Here," she said, handing me a glass containing pink coloured liquid, a straw and an umbrella. "It's Red Banana."

I sat up and took the glass from her. "What's in it?"

"Vodka, banana liqueur and strawberry juice."

I took a sip through the straw. "Mmm, it's quite nice. A bit sweet and sickly though. I don't think I could drink more than a couple of these in a row."

We sat for a few minutes in silence. Jayne was one of the few people I could sit in silence with comfortably. "Shall we go to Sousse tomorrow?" Jayne suggested.

"Yeah, why not. We'll ask reception to order a taxi for us, shall we?"

Jayne nodded whilst sipping her cocktail through the straw.

∞

The next day we got a taxi into Sousse as planned. We followed the signs to the Medina and as we entered the market place, a young Tunisian approached us. "Hello," he said, smiling broadly at us.

"Hello," we both replied, slowing down but without stopping.

"I see you get out of my brother's taxi," he continued, now beginning to walk along beside us. "I show you the best places to go where you get best quality." The young Tunisian then walked on ahead towards a jewellery shop. "This shop sells good quality jewellery. No fakes. And you will get no hassle in this shop." He led us into the shop and like sheep we followed him.

The shop-keeper approached us as we entered, smiling just as broadly as the young Tunisian who had led us there. "These are English ladies," he introduced us. "I show them your shop."

The shop-keeper was older and shorter, but with a better grasp of the English language than the young Tunisian. "Hello, please have a look," he said. "We have gold and silver. No fakes." Jayne and I began to browse. "Your first time in Tunisia?"

"Yes," we replied in unison.

"You here with family?"

"No it's just us two," we replied.

"You like a drink?" Jayne and I looked at one another. "No pressure to buy. Just hospitality. We have Fanta, water, tea?"

"Just water, please," we both replied.

He spoke to his assistant who disappeared, returning moments later with two small bottles of water. "Please take a seat," said the shop-keeper, gesturing towards a small wooden two-seater bench covered with a large tapestry cushion.

We did as we were told. "That's it, just relax," said the shop-keeper. "I show you some jewellery. Special prices today. End of season." He then brought out two large black boxes with glass lids. One contained gold jewellery and the other contained silver. "These are all genuine gold. Good quality." The shop-keeper lifted one of the gold bracelets out of the box and fastened it around Jayne's wrist. "You like this one?"

"Yes, it's lovely," said Jayne.

"How much you pay for this in England?"

"Oh, I don't know," said Jayne. "I never buy real gold. I can't afford it."

"It's very expensive in England, no? But here you pay just one hundred and seventy dinars. Not pounds, but dinars," he emphasised.

"How much is that?" Jayne muttered to me.

Before we could work it out, the shop-keeper produced a large calculator, pressed a few buttons, then said, "that's sixty in your English pounds."

"Sorry, but that's too much," said Jayne.

"Okay, I give you discount as it's end of season. I will give it to you for a hundred and forty-five dinars." Again he pressed a few buttons on his calculator. "That's fifty-two in your English pounds."

"That's still too much," said Jayne, beginning to try to undo the clasp of the bracelet.

The shop-keeper placed his hand on hers, indicating he did not want Jayne to remove the bracelet. "Okay, what will you pay for it?" he asked.

"Oh, I don't know," said Jayne. "Say........thirty pounds?"

"No, no," he said. "That's stupid price!"

"Well I think that's all I can afford at the moment," said Jayne. "And besides, I also need to buy presents."

"I take credit card."

"I haven't got any cards with me," explained Jayne, and I knew she was telling the truth.

"I know what you're thinking," the shop-keeper's tone was a little softer now. "You think, you should not spend money on yourself, but you work hard all year. No? You deserve to buy something nice for yourself, something to remind you of Tunisia."

"Yes, but....."

"I tell you what, I will sell you two bracelets for price of one," he interrupted. He then lifted another gold bracelet from the box, and before I realised, was fastening it around my wrist. "Two bracelets for two hundred and fifty dinars. That's only ninety pounds."

"I'm sorry," I said, taking the bracelet back off, "but we'd rather look around first and think about it."

"You must buy now," he said, and his tone was now more earnest. "I can only sell for this special price if you buy now."

"I'm sorry, but I do not buy from the first shop I see," I said, standing up. "We will come back if we decide to buy from you."

I was already walking out the shop before Jayne managed to take her bracelet off and stand up. "Why you leave?" the shop-keeper asked, and there was a tinge of aggression in his voice. "I gave you hospitality." Jayne followed me out of the shop. "Why you not speak?" he shouted after us.

"Carry on walking," I muttered to Jayne, feeling just a little bit shook up.

We ventured deeper into the Medina, along narrow streets lined with small open-fronted shops, the shop-keepers sat or stood outside displaying their wares, trying to entice us in. "Hello, lovely ladies.....Come in!.... Let me show you my shop.....Cheaper than Asda price." We soon realised that if we stopped to look, nothing was priced and we would have to go through the long and tedious ordeal of bartering until both parties reached a mutually acceptable price. We would also end up buying something we didn't really want or buy more than we intended. So eventually we developed the strategy of adopting a confident stride and an intent expression, without even glancing sideways in case we caught someone's eye, suggesting there was somewhere far more important we needed to be, until we escaped unscathed out the other end.

We managed to arrive back at our hotel in time for a late lunch. I chose stuffed zucchini with rice and salad from the buffet style menu. At a neighbouring table sat the family of the little boy in the Mickey Mouse hat. The boy's mother smiled at me as I caught her eye, and I smiled back. A few moments later, she was chatting along to me. She asked about our visit to Sousse, informing me that they were planning to visit on the Wednesday which was in two days' time. I remarked on their little boy's Mickey Mouse hat, which evoked a huge smile on the part of the little boy, revealing a mouthful of perfect little baby white teeth. "The trouble is, he never wants to take it off now," laughed his mother.

As we left the restaurant and began heading back to our room, the Tunisian from the photo booth practically jumped out on us. "I take nice photos of you, only three dinars each?"

"Not just now," I said. "We are going to get changed for the beach."

"Four o'clock tomorrow, you come here, and I take nice photos? By the pool, on the beach."

"Okay," I said. Three dinars seemed reasonable.

After we got changed in our room into our swimwear and sarongs, we made our way to the beach which was directly overlooked by our hotel. There were plenty of free sunbeds, so we chose two that were close to the water's edge, shaded by a large parasol. I lowered the back rest and lay down flat on my back, closing my eyes. As I listened to the rhythmic sound of the tide rushing to the shore, and then retreating, I thought, the twins would have loved this; building castles and looking for baby jellyfish washed up on the beautiful, soft sandy beach. In fact, I wished they were with me right now.

It was almost five o'clock and we began to make our way back to our room to get changed for dinner. "Look!" said Jayne suddenly. "That couple are just leaving the photo booth. Shall we ask them if they recommend the photographer?"

"Yeah, good idea," I said. We walked towards them as they were heading our way. "Excuse me. Would you mind if we just asked you something....about the photographer?"

"No," replied the woman. "What would you like to know?"

"Well, would you recommend him, or does he try to pressurise you into spending more than you intended, if you know what I mean?"

"Yeah, I know exactly what you mean," she smiled.

"It's just that we've agreed to meet him tomorrow at four, but we're beginning to have second thoughts."

"Well put it this way," the woman began. "He took over six hundred photos. In the end we had to say quite firmly, 'no more photos.' Then we had to look through them all and choose which ones we wanted, which took forever. We ended up by spending seventy pounds."

"Really?"

"Don't get me wrong," the woman continued, "they were nice photos, but if you only want half a dozen, you need to be very firm about that."

After we thanked the couple for their advice and they had walked away, we both said what we were both clearly thinking. Basically, rather than having to be assertive and insist that we only want half a dozen photos at most, we would just not turn up. The thing is, it would mean avoiding the photographer for the rest of the holiday. Besides, did Jayne and I really want professional photos taken of us? As a couple that would be weird. On our own would be sad.

∞

The next day we bumped into the photographer a couple of times when he reminded us that we had a photo shoot booked with him at four o'clock (like we were likely to forget). At around three thirty we were back in our room. We decided to sit and sunbathe on our terrace for a while before getting ready for dinner. Alongside ours and the two hotel rooms adjacent to ours, was a small swimming pool, seemingly for the private use of the three rooms. There were several of these swim-up pools situated around the hotel grounds, part of the new design I suspected. Jayne and I sat on the white plastic chairs on our terrace, playing cards at the white plastic table. I could just see the larger pool from where we were sitting, a large patch of green in-between. Jayne had made us both a cup of coffee with the limited tea and coffee making facilities in our room.

"Oh my God!" I exclaimed suddenly.

"What is it?" Jayne couldn't see what I could see because she had her back to the pool.

"It's the photographer," I said.

"Has he seen us?"

"I'm not sure……" I said, vaguely. "Yes, I think he's spotted us! He's heading this way!" Both Jayne and I jumped up from our seats. My chair lifted slightly off the floor, due to being stuck to my sweaty thighs before dropping back down again. I then almost tripped over the chair in my haste. I was just about to enter our room via the sliding glass patio doors when I heard a splash and felt something wet spray my back. I turned around to see Jayne spluttering about in the water. The photographer had stopped and was watching the scene, wearing a somewhat bewildered expression.

"Are you okay?" I asked, my voice beginning to quiver on the brink of laughter.

"Bloody hell! Bloody hell!" exclaimed Jayne. "I'll have to wash my hair now!"

I began to laugh, partly because Jayne hardly ever swore. I walked to the edge of the pool in an attempt to help her out. The pool wasn't deep. Jayne was now standing up and the water barely met her chest, but the water had completely engulfed her when she fell, so that her hair was flat against her head, water running down her face. A drowned rat came to mind.

CHAPTER FORTY-NINE

Fortunately we didn't see the photographer again that day, and the next day we embarked on a two day trip to the Sahara. As our coach travelled along the long and winding dusty roads, I gazed out of the window, half-dreaming and half-listening to the Tunisian tour guide as he gave a detailed account of Tunisian history and culture into a microphone at the front of the coach. In between rows of olive trees, some hundreds of years old, stood small half-built houses with tiny windows and no roofs, and dilapidated cafes with sheep and goats hanging upside down outside ready to cook and eat.

Our first stop was at El Djem where we were privileged to see the most unspoilt monument in Tunisia, the Roman Coloseum. I am embarrassed to admit that although I like to consider myself to be cultured, looking around ancient ruins I usually find only mildly interesting at best, and extremely tedious at worst. However, this was different, and not just because I knew the film 'Gladiator' was filmed there (albeit digitially remastered). Like everything else I was to experience on this tour, El Jem was extremely impressive. We were encouraged to venture underground where the Gladiators prepared and the animals were kept prior to their release into the arena. We then began to climb the large uneven stone steps to reach each level of the gallery. "Sorry, Jayne, I can't climb any higher," I panted. Jayne was the same age as me, in fact three months older, but she was obviously fitter than me. "If you reach the top, wave down to me and I'll take a photo of you," I said, as I began my descent.

Eventually Jayne climbed as high as she could go and I could just make her out waving down at me as I stood in the centre of the arena. I took a photo of her, then waved back, hoping she would reciprocate. *They'll make brilliant photos,* I thought to myself.

After El Jem, we were back on the road. As the journey to our next destination was going to be quite some time, our tour guide passed around some Ramadan cake which our driver had apparently brought for us. "It's flavoured with orange blossom," explained our guide as he offered the basket of cake for us to sample. Jayne and I both lifted a piece of cake from the basket, thanking him in anticipation of something different but hopefully delicious. As we bit into the dry cake, Jayne and I both screwed up our faces.

"It's horrible," I muttered to Jayne under my breath. "It tastes like cheap perfume."

"What should we do with it?" asked Jayne.

"We'll just throw it in the rubbish bag when he's not looking," I said. We both giggled like naughty children.

"You like it?" our guide asked us, smiling broadly as he made his way back along the passengers on the other side of the coach.

"Oh, yes, very nice," we both said in unison, holding the cake up to prove we were actually eating it. As soon as his back was turned, Jayne passed me her cake which along with mine, I promptly threw in the carrier bag hanging on the arm of my seat.

We eventually arrived at a camel station in Douz on the fringes of the Sahara desert. After we disembarked, we were all led into a room where we donned the typical robes and head-scarves that were reminiscent of *Lawrence of Arabia*. We were then led outside to where the camels were waiting patiently. Our guide had informed us that camels were the subject of a great deal of poetry and they had seven and a half thousand words in Arabic connected to camels. Our guide had also told us, "when we get back on the coach, none of you will mind how bad you smell because we will all smell like camels."

"No chance of us pulling then?" I said to Jayne.

"Oh I dunno," said Jayne. "Didn't our guide say that camels were treasured? Perhaps that's what Tunisian men are most drawn to: women who smell like camels."

We both laughed as we stood waiting our turn to mount the camels who were waiting patiently on the sand.

"How many?" asked one of the men with the camels.

"Two," we said in unison.

"Come here," we were instructed. Two camels were kneeling behind one another, tethered together by a rope.

"You can have the camel in front," said Jayne. "I'll have the other one. He looks smaller."

"Okay," I said as I walked around the camels so that I could mount the one in front from the left side. I raised my right leg over the camel's back and eased myself into its saddle behind the hump, holding tightly onto the handle with both hands. Almost immediately, the camel stood up and I let out a squeal as I tipped forward. Suddenly I was up very high looking down at the camel's head.

As the caravan of camels ambled its way across the sand, the red sun began to set. Within a few short minutes the sun had disappeared from view, leaving a smudge of red on the horizon. As we ventured further and further into the desert, I turned around to speak to Jayne. "I'm getting saddle sore!" I laughed.

The man leading our camels then came to an abrupt stop. "You like me to take photo?" he asked.

"Yes, please," I said, trying to retrieve my camera from the pocket in my jeans. I switched it on and then leaned forward to give him the camera. Jayne and I smiled as we had our photo taken.

"That should be a good one for the album," said Jayne.

The man handed the camera back to me and we then continued our journey. Despite the discomfort, there was really something very relaxing about riding across the desert sands. I would never have believed it before then, but the camels had a certain grace and serenity about them, and despite what we had been told previously, I didn't even notice an unpleasant aroma. "You want to gallop now?" the man leading our camels asked over his shoulder.

"God, no!" Jayne exclaimed. "No galloping, please! I'll never stay on!"

By the time we arrived back at the camel station it was dark. We paid and handed over our robes and scarves, before getting back on to the coach. Less than fifteen minutes later we were at the hotel we were to stay in that night. We were shown to our rooms where we showered and changed ready for dinner. As we helped ourselves to the buffet, we noticed an old lady dressed in traditional garments sat on the floor in the corner of the dining room, making bread. I had pumpkin stew and tadzin, washed down with a glass of celtia. After dinner, Jayne and I had a Turkish coffee in the bar before retiring to our room. It felt so good to slide into bed, the cool sheets against my skin and the soft pillow under my head. We lay in our beds in the dark chatting about our day before settling down to sleep. We had been promised a four o'clock alarm call the following morning as we had to be ready to leave the hotel at five. "It's early," our guide had said, "but I promise you a truly wondrous sight that when you see it, you will think was definitely worth it."

It was still dark when we left the hotel the following morning. Our guide was quiet for most of the journey, allowing the passengers to catch up on their sleep if they so wished. By the time the coach finally stopped it was just past 6.30. The wondrous sight we were promised certainly met our hopes and expectations. We watched in awe as the sun rose over the salt lakes, that stretched out before us like a vast sea of snow. Everyone was taking photos, precious moments fixed in time with the click of a shutter. "Wow!" I exclaimed. "This is really something special, isn't it Jayne?" Jayne just nodded, seemingly lost for words for once in her life. "I'm so glad we came."

Our next stop was at a little café where we waited for a different kind of transport altogether: nine Mitsubishi land cruises which were going to take us for a ride over the sand dunes. So it was back to the Sahara for us.

As the convoy of jeeps wound their way further and further into the desert, the clumps of dry grass that goats, sheep and camels grazed on became more and more sparse until they were non-existent. Then the jeeps began to turn off the dusty make-shift road towards the sand dunes. Apart from the driver, there were six passengers in our jeep. Next to the driver sat one of the men from our tour group, behind them sat Jayne and I, as well as another woman who I presumed was the front passenger's wife. "These are my three wives," he joked with the driver, gesturing towards the three of us sat behind them. Behind Jayne and I sat another couple who we assumed were also husband and wife.

Before us rose a small mountain of sand. As the driver headed towards it, I thought to myself, *surely he's not going to drive up it?* But he did. And as he did so, I gripped onto Jayne's arm as the jeep tipped to the side, feeling as though it were going to topple over. A unison of high-pitched shrieks pierced the warm dry air, which were immediately followed by laughter as we descended the other side of the dune. But as soon as we had composed ourselves, the driver headed towards an even steeper dune. As he drove up it, the jeep became almost vertical. As more shrieks filled the air, the driver emitted an almost maniacal laugh. Despite the two large cracks in the windscreen, I kept telling myself, *he's an experienced driver. He knows what he's doing.* Then the jeep paused momentarily at the top, like at the summit of a rollercoaster before the inevitable drop down the other side. "Oh my God!" cried Jayne, half with fear, half with laughter.

"I wanna get off!" I laughed as we descended. I continued laughing so much I began choking on the dry dusty air.

After our exhilarating ride over the sand dunes (and it was exhilarating, scary but exhilarating), we headed towards the Chebika. As I gazed out of the window, fossilised shells glistened with the sun's rays like a trillion tiny shards of glass. Finally, we reached the palm swathed oasis at the foot of the Atlas Mountains. Some locals had their stalls set up outside selling jewellery, quartz, toy camels and freshly squeezed orange juice. Jayne and I followed the line of tourists who made their way rather precariously through a narrow path in the rocks. Tiny frogs with high-pitched voices like little dogs yapping, hopped in and out of the trickle of water that meandered its way around the rocks. When we emerged the other side, any concerns we may have had about health and safety, were dispelled immediately by the sight we beheld. For there before us stood a beautiful waterfall, tall and majestic. The natural spring water fell into a small turquoise lake, almost iridescent in the glow of the midday sun. We could walk right up to the edge of the lake. I dangled my fingers in the water. "It's warm," I said. Jayne followed my example, bending down to touch the water.

"Let me take a photo of you," I said, taking out my camera. Jayne posed at the water's edge, the waterfall behind her.

"Now let me take one of you," said Jayne.

Before we left, I took one last look around me. A mental panoramic shot. I knew our photographs would never do this place justice. "So beautiful," I muttered to myself. "So beautiful".

CHAPTER FIFTY

It was the last day of our holiday. Our flight wasn't until midnight and our transfer coach wasn't due to pick us up until nine o'clock that evening. So, Jayne and I decided to soak up as much of the Tunisian sun as we could before our departure. Quite surprisingly it seemed to be the hottest day of our holiday. We relaxed on the sunbeds by the pool, me with my book and Jayne with her puzzles. The place was now almost deserted. Most of the tourists had already left for the airport to catch an earlier flight. It was so peaceful, a perfect end to our holiday. Even the sea was calm that day.

After we had returned from our trip to the Sahara, we received news about a suicide bomb attack that had occurred the day before on the beach in Sousse, close to the Riadh Palms hotel. Immediately I thought of the little boy in the Mickey Mouse hat and his family. I hadn't seen them since we had spoken in the restaurant the day before we left for our trip. Fortunately, however, the news also confirmed that no one was hurt, apart from the suicide bomber who apparently blew himself up on the empty beach after being chased away from the hotel.

As our plane began its descent, panic gripped me like a hawk grips its prey, so tenaciously it almost took my breath away. I knew no one from home would contact me unless they really had to, so I had no idea what had been happening while I had been away. Had Adam had the operation? If he had, had he actually survived it? If he had, was he paralysed? I knew he'd rather be dead than that. It was easier to push these thoughts to the back of my mind while I was thousands of miles away, but now I was nearly home, it had all suddenly become very real again.

When I arrived home, I telephoned Ben to let him know that I had arrived safely and to get an update on his father's situation.

"Did you have a nice time?" Ben asked.

"Yeah, we had a lovely time, thanks." Then after a suitable pause, "How's Dad?"

"They operated on him," Ben explained. "And the operation was apparently a success. He's still very confused though. Although they tell me that's to be expected."

I let out a sigh of relief. "Oh good, I'm glad the operation went okay."

"I gotta admit Mum, I was a bit worried. He was in theatre for almost eleven hours. I thought there must have been complications. But apparently not."

"Have you been to see him?" I asked.

"Yes once," replied Ben. "I not sure he knew who I was though."

"What ward is he on?" I asked.

"Ward 10. I have the telephone number if you want it? And the visiting times."

I wrote down the ward's telephone number and visiting times. "I'll probably visit tomorrow," I said.

∞

The next day I visited Adam at the hospital. He was on his own in a side room. As I entered, he turned his head towards me and smiled. It was good to see him sat up in bed without a collar on or blocks strapped to each side of his head. He did not look entirely well though. His complexion was very pale, almost grey. "Hi Fay! It's so good to see you." At least he recognised me.

"How are you?" I asked.

"Well I could be better," he said. "The doctor tells me I should make a full recovery though. In time."

"I think you've been very lucky," I said. "It could have been a lot worse."

"I know."

"So has it made you think?" I asked. "About the future I mean."

"Yeah it has," said Adam. "I realise I have to stop drinking if I want to get you back."

"You need to stop drinking for *yourself*," I said. "Not just for me."

"I know." But I wondered if he really did know that. If he really believed that. Deep down. "I've been having these really vivid dreams," Adam went on…. "Sometimes I don't know what's real and what isn't. I dreamt last night that my Mum was still alive. She was in this room and talking to me. I was convinced when I woke up that it was real. But it couldn't have been, could it?"

"No, it couldn't have been," I said.

Adam didn't mention my holiday so neither did I. To talk about it would have just seemed like rubbing salt into his wounds. Instead I continued to ask him the usual mundane and predictable questions one asks when you're visiting someone in hospital.

"Are you eating well?" I asked. "How's the food?"

"I haven't got much of an appetite," said Adam. "Especially as they insist on giving me food all mushed up." I glanced at the sign on the wall behind Adam's bed which read: *pureed diet only. Observe whilst eating.*

"Why's that?" I asked.

"Just because I started choking one day when I was eating a particularly horrible meal, they think I can't swallow properly."

"Well they're probably just being cautious," I suggested. I noticed a zimmer frame in the corner of the room, so in order to change the subject, I asked: "have they got you walking yet?"

I've managed to walk a couple of steps with the frame," said Adam. "I'm not allowed to try walking on my own yet."

"No, well that sounds sensible enough," I said. "Have you been having physiotherapy?"

"Yeah, every day," said Adam. "That's a bit of a pain though."

"You must let them help you," I said. "I hope you're not being difficult?"

"No, of course I'm not."

At that moment, a pretty young woman wearing a white dress, similar to a nurse's uniform, entered the room, pushing a tea trolley. "Would you like a drink, Adam?" She seemed cheerful enough.

"Yes please," said Adam. "A cup of tea would be nice. Strong……"

"………with one sugar," said the young woman, finishing Adam's sentence for him.

"That's right," said Adam jovially.

After the young woman had placed a cup of tea within Adam's reach on the overbed table and left the room, I said "she seems nice."

"Yeah, they're all pretty nice here," said Adam.

Before long, visiting time was over. Partly with regret and partly with relief, I said my good-byes.

"When will you come again?" Adam asked.

"I'm not sure," I said. "It's a long way, and I'm back at work tomorrow."

"Please come as soon as you can," he said. "It's very lonely here on my own. The days are so long without any visitors."

"Ben came to see you," I reminded him. "Do you remember that?"

Adam looked pensive for a moment, then said "yeah, of course I remember." But I wondered if he really did.

"Has John been to see you yet?" I asked.

"No," said Adam. "I don't think so."

I knew John hadn't visited. I had spoken to John on the phone the day before, after I had spoken to Ben. "I don't see much point in visiting him if he's away with the fairies," John had said. I suppose I couldn't really blame him. He had been there for Adam far more over the years than Adam had been there for him. But Adam was still his brother. Nothing could ever change that.

∞

I lied about being back at work the next day. I had one more day left of my holiday and I didn't want to spend it travelling backwards and forwards to the hospital again. As I drove into town, a felt a pang of guilt. I visualised Adam on his own in that little room. Feeling isolated, lonely, perhaps afraid. I tried my hardest to banish this vision from my mind.

Fortunately, I found a parking space fairly easily. As it was a weekday, the town was quieter than usual. I would normally only go into town on a Saturday, but I needed to go to the Bank. As I walked along the high street, everything was as it was before I went away. People going about their usual business. I had only been away a week, but it seemed much longer. I used to love going away, but always loved coming back almost as much. Back to normality. I used to love normality. But not anymore. I wanted anything but. Every familiar place and every familiar face reminded me of what had changed for me and Adam, when everything around us seemed to have remained the same. Even people's laughter cut through me like a knife. Things that used to make me smile now made me want to cry.

From inside my handbag, I heard the familiar, yet what had now become the ominous ringtone of my mobile phone. I slipped my hand into the side pocket. The screen read: unknown caller. I pressed the answer button and lifted the phone to my ear. "Hello?"

"Hi, Debbie, it's Adam!"

"What?"

"I was wondering if you were still coming to see me today?" asked Adam.

"No, I said I wasn't coming to see you until the weekend. I'm back at work today," I lied.

"Oh, sorry, Debbie. I'm getting mixed up with the days."

"Why are you calling me Debbie?" I asked. But my question was met with silence. "Adam! Did you hear what I said?"

"Yes."

"What's my name?" I asked him.

"Debbie," he replied.

"No, it's not. I'm Fay, don't you remember?"

"Oh, sorry, I thought I was talking to Debbie."

"Why would you be talking to Debbie?" I asked, beginning to feel quite exasperated. "As far as I know, you haven't seen her in years."

"Oh, sorry," Adam apologised again. "They've confused me, telling me it was Debbie on the phone."

"Why would they say that?"

"I don't know."

"Besides, you rang me!" This conversation was getting ridiculous.

"Did I?"

"Yes," I said, emphatically. I exhaled a deep sigh, realising it was best just to change the subject now. "How are you, anyway?"

"Getting better, I think. Bored out of my mind though," said Adam. Then the tone of his voice changed, suddenly charged with a much stronger feeling. "God, I miss you so much."

Then I wondered if it was really me or Debbie that he missed. "I only saw you yesterday," I said.

"I know."

"Is there anything you want me to bring when I visit?" I asked, changing the subject. "Perhaps something to read?"

"Yeah, a newspaper or something, if you don't mind," said Adam.

"Okay, I can do that."

CHAPTER FIFTY-ONE

When I visited Adam at the weekend, he seemed less confused. As I entered his room, I found him watching a small flat screened television which was fixed to the wall opposite his bed. He turned the volume down when he saw me. "Hi, Fay!" said Adam, I'm so glad you came. I was beginning to think you weren't coming." At least he was calling me Fay and not Debbie.

"I'm not late am I?" I said.

"No, I don't think so. I was just worried."

"You look a bit better today," I said. I glanced at the sign behind the bed which read: *normal diet*. "I see you're not on pureed food anymore."

"Yes, thank God," said Adam.

I also noticed that the drip he had been attached to had now been removed.

"I've got some documents for you to sign," I said. "For the solicitor." I opened the large envelope I had been carrying under my arm and took out some papers. "He said he will need to see you before the contracts are exchanged though. I think he needs to be satisfied that you have consented to this and not been coerced into it."

"Well, it's not really what I want," said Adam. "You know that."

"What you want is things to go back to the way they were," I said. "But that's not going to happen. I can't afford to keep up the repayments any longer, so If we don't sell the house, it will end up being re-possessed and we'll both lose everything. Is that really what you want?"

"No of course not."

"Then sign the documents," I said. "And please don't tell the solicitor you don't want to sell when he sees you. If you sabotage this, I'll never forgive you."

Perhaps this threat was a form of coercion. But I couldn't risk this sale falling through. And it wouldn't be in either of our best interests if it did.

∞

The sale of the house went through pretty quickly after that. I had to put most of Adam's stuff in storage, apart from his clothes and some basic essentials. He now had priority banding on the council housing list. Our house was sold, but even if it hadn't been, Adam couldn't live there anymore. He needed ground floor accommodation now. He couldn't risk falling down the stairs again.

It was the 20th of December, just five days before Christmas. Adam had been transferred to our local hospital for convalescence. Although I doubt that anyone would wish to be in hospital at Christmas, I was relieved that they had no plans to discharge Adam before the New Year. The council flat he had now been promised wouldn't be ready for him to move into until then. Besides, Christmas is definitely not the best time of year for an alcoholic who is clinging precariously to the wagon that's already lost one wheel.

I found Adam in the day room, sat watching TV. "Hi, Fay," he smiled as I approached him. "Thank you for coming. It's so boring here. I feel like I'm going stir crazy."

"I've brought you some more Dr Pepper," I said, taking three small bottles out of a carrier bag. "And a newspaper."

"Thanks."

"How are you feeling?" I asked.

"They're discharging me," said Adam.

"What?" I said, incredulously. "When?"

"On Monday."

"But that's the day before Christmas Eve."

"I know," said Adam.

"But where are you going to stay?"

"I don't know."

"Excuse me!" I called out to a nurse who was passing by.

"Yes?" she said as she turned towards me.

"Is it right that you're planning to discharge Adam on Monday?"

"Yes I believe so."

"But he's got nowhere to live," I said. "Surely you can't discharge him if he's got nowhere to live?"

"The Doctor's seen Adam today and has said he's medically fit for discharge."

I couldn't quite believe my ears. Only yesterday I was told not to worry as they had no plans to discharge Adam until after Christmas. "I'll have to ring the Council," I said to Adam. "See if they can get some emergency accommodation for you."

"Can't I stay with you?" Adam asked.

"I don't think that's such a good idea, do you?"

After I left the ward, I immediately phoned the council on my mobile. I was put through to Sally who seemed rather unsympathetic. However, she said she would contact Adam as soon as she was able to find some emergency accommodation for him.

A couple of hours later Adam phoned me. "Darren has offered to put me up until I get something more permanent."

"Whose Darren?" I asked.

"He's someone I met at A.A."

"Oh, so another alcoholic?" I exclaimed.

"A *recovering* alcoholic," corrected Adam. "I think it was very generous of him actually."

"Yeah, I suppose," I conceded. "What about the emergency housing?"

"They could only offer me bed and breakfast twenty miles away. I didn't want to go twenty miles away, especially as I no longer have a car."

I was actually quite relieved that Adam had found somewhere to stay and in a way, I thought, Darren might actually turn out to be a positive role model for Adam. But what Adam failed to inform me was that Darren would be going to his sister's for Christmas, so Adam would actually be alone over the festive period.

"Will you be okay?" I asked.

"Yeah, I'll just buy a ready meal for myself," said Adam. "Then chill out in front of the tele.....it's no big deal."

But I felt guilty. I had planned to spend Christmas day with Ben, Anita and the twins. Somehow it seemed wrong that Adam would be spending the day alone now. And I was worried. Worried that he'd get melancholy and then have a drink. But of course he wouldn't stop at one drink. In no time at all, he'd be back where he started.

So after some consideration and discussion with Ben and Anita, I made Adam an offer. "If you like, you can come to me Christmas Eve and stay the night," I said. "In the spare room of course." Adam's eyes began to light up. "Then Christmas day, we'll go to Ben and Anita's for dinner. After we come back to the flat, you can stay the night again. Then you can go back to Darren's boxing day."

For once, Adam seemed lost for words. Eventually he spoke. "You have no idea how happy that makes me," said Adam, beaming.

"But if you let me down, that'll be it," I warned. "If you drink, you will have to go, no question about that. And I won't forgive you again. Not this time." I felt it was important I made myself perfectly clear.

"I won't let you down," said Adam. "I promise."

CHAPTER FIFTY-TWO

It was Christmas Eve. The shopping was done. The presents were wrapped, and I had placed Adam's under the tree. I was actually looking forward to spending Christmas with him. This may be the turning point, I thought. I didn't love him anymore, at least not the way I used to. But I did miss his company sometimes, despite all the pain he had caused me. Nevertheless, I was almost too afraid to hope. Afraid because I didn't want to be let down yet again. I wasn't sure that I could cope with another disappointment. I was just putting on my boots when there was a knock on the door. I wasn't working that day and had arranged to meet Jayne for lunch and a drink.

I opened the door to find Adam standing on the doorstep. "What are you doing here?" I asked. "I wasn't expecting you until later."

"Darren's already left for his sister's. I thought I might as well come up now, if that's okay?"

"Well I was just on my way out," I said, stepping back to let Adam in through the door. "I won't be back for a couple of hours."

"That's no problem. If you don't mind me just sitting in your flat watching the tele?"

"No, I suppose that'll be all right," I said.

"These are your presents," said Adam, handing me a carrier bag containing three presents wrapped in gold paper. They even had matching bows attached to them. I wondered if he had in fact wrapped them himself.

"Thank you," I said, taking the presents out of the bag and placing them under the tree. I didn't say so, but I would have preferred it if Adam had bought something for the twins rather than me. "Help yourself to a drink. The kitchen's through there," I said. "Not alcohol of course. I haven't got any of that."

"You didn't need to say that," said Adam. "I have no intention of drinking."

Adam dropped down on the settee with a bump, then as he looked up at me, I noticed his eyes. They were glazed over. Suddenly a horrible thought entered my head but I dismissed it immediately. I needed to be sure though. "You haven't been drinking, have you?"

"No, of course not!" exclaimed Adam with indignation. "Is this what it's going to be like all over Christmas?"

"No," I said, emphatically. "I won't say another word on the subject."

Jayne was already waiting outside the café when I crossed the road from the car park. "Sorry I'm late," I said. "Adam turned up and......."

"Oh, no!" interrupted Jayne. "He hadn't been drinking, had he?"

"No, he hadn't," I assured her. "At least I don't think so."

"You don't think so?" echoed Jayne.

"No, he hadn't. He definitely hadn't. He'd be stupid to do that." I wasn't sure who I was trying to convince, Jayne or myself.

I was gone for a couple of hours. I had bought something else for Adam as I'd only really bought him a token present and he seemed to have made a bit more of an effort than I had. It was something quite functional. A new dressing gown. But he needed one, and it was good quality. I had also bought some wine to take to Ben and Anita's, but immediately wondered whether I should have done. In fact, I was beginning to wonder if having Christmas dinner at Ben's was a good idea after all. Although Ben and Anita weren't big drinkers, they would no doubt like a glass of wine or two with their dinner. I wouldn't want them to feel as though they couldn't have a drink.

As I opened the door of the flat, I could hear the television. "I'm back!" I called out, but there was no response. The first thing I noticed when I entered the sitting room was Adam, asleep on the settee. He was still sat upright, his head to one side and his mouth agape. Then I noticed the empty bottle of brandy on the coffee table, and my heart sank.

I walked over to Adam, laying my hand on his shoulder to shake him. "Adam. Adam!" His eyelids parted but all I could see was the whites of his eyes which were rolled back inside their sockets. Then I noticed the large wet patch on his jeans. He had wet himself. I shook him again, with both hands and more roughly this time. "Adam! Adam!" I shouted in his ear. "I want you to go!"

But my words were just met with a groan. Suddenly I felt distraught. I didn't want Adam here. I wanted him out of my flat. Now! Frustration quickly rose within me like a volcano ready to erupt. I then punched him as hard as I could in his chest. He groaned again, more loudly this time. Part of me almost wished Adam would fight me, hit me back. He had promised he would never hit me again, and he hadn't. But right now, I think I would have preferred that to this. I would have done almost anything at that point to have the old Adam back, instead of this pathetic shell of a person.

Not knowing what else to do, I picked up the phone and rang the Police.

"So you let him in?" asked the woman at the other end of the phone. "It's not really appropriate for the Police to remove him when you've invited him into your home."

"But I don't want him here now," I said, getting more and more exasperated by the second. "I want him to leave but he won't go."

"Did you say he was intoxicated?"

"Yes. He's practically unconscious."

"So how do you know he's refusing to go? It might be better if you wait for him to sober up, don't you think?" she suggested.

"But I want him to go now! It's my flat and I don't want him here! He was only welcome providing he didn't drink. I trusted him. I would never have let him in if I thought he was going to do this to me again. You have no idea what I've been through......." My voice was shaking now. I could no longer hold back the tears.

"Okay," sighed the woman at the other end of the phone. "A Police car is on it's way."

"Thank you," I just managed to get out in between my sobs.

It seemed ages before the Police arrived, by which time, Adam was more alert and began speaking to me, albeit in a slurred voice. I walked to the door as I heard the sound of car doors slamming outside. "Thank you for coming," I said when I opened the door to two Police officers in full uniform, who then followed me through to the sitting room. I was now feeling more composed. In fact I had began to wonder if calling the police was something of an over-reaction.

"Oh, hello," said Adam, with a smile, as though the arrival of the Police was nothing out of the ordinary.

"Hello, Sir," said one of the Police officers. "It's Adam, isn't it?" Adam nodded. "So, what's been going on here then?"

"Nothing," said Adam, innocently.

"Nothing?" echoed the same Police officer. "Apparently you've been drinking. And apparently you're not supposed to drink.....not anymore."

"No," said Adam. "I haven't been drinking. I know I'm not supposed to drink."

Both the faces of the Police officers broke out into ironic smiles. Now it was the younger Police officer's turn to speak...."What's that then?"

"What's what?" Was Adam deliberately being obtuse?

"That empty brandy bottle on the coffee table," was the Police officer's reply.

"Oh that," said Adam. "I must admit, you've got me there." Adam grimaced as though he were a naughty boy getting caught for stealing apples, or some other misdemeanour.

"Well the thing is," the Police officer continued, "your ex-wife doesn't want you here."

She's not my ex-wife," corrected Adam. "We're still married."

"Okay, but you're separated aren't you?"

"That wasn't my decision. I never wanted us to split up."

"That's not important," said the Police officer. "The fact is this is Fay's flat and she wants you to leave."

"She invited me," protested Adam.

"Yeah, but that was before you got pissed out of your head," I interjected. Both Police men were looking at me now, so I felt I now needed to explain. "Adam's an alcoholic. I said he could spend Christmas here as I felt sorry for him having to spend it alone. But it was only under the condition that he didn't drink." I felt I needed to go on. "He's just come out of hospital. He was in for ten weeks after falling down the stairs and breaking his neck when he was drunk. He's lucky to be alive."

Both the Police officers nodded with understanding. "Okay, are we going to stand up then," said the older of the two.

"Well you're already standing up, aren't you?" came Adam's quick-witted reply. However, his humour was wasted on the Police officers.

"Come on, then," they cajoled, as they stood either side of Adam, attempting to grasp hold of his arms to help him up.

But Adam just shook them off. "I can do it!" he insisted.

"Okay. Go on then," said the Police officers, stepping back.

Adam began rocking back and forth in an attempt to gather some momentum so that he could stand. He lifted himself up by his arms just a few inches, but then fell back down again. "Let us help you," suggested the older Policeman. Adam acquiesced.

"Is this his bag?" asked the younger Policeman, pointing at the rucksack on the floor.

"Yes it is," I said, lifting it up and handing it to him.

"Where am I going?" asked Adam as he tottered towards the door.

"Where has he been staying?" asked the older Police officer.

"At a friend's house," I replied. "I'm afraid I don't know his address, but Adam should."

"Have you got a key to get in?" asked the Police officer.

"Yeah, in my pocket," said Adam. He began fumbling in his pockets. I was worried at first as he didn't seem to be able to find the key. Then something fell out of his pocket, and we heard the sound of metal against wood as the key landed on the wood flooring. Adam bent forward to pick it up but the policemen had to grab hold of him as he almost fell flat on his face.

"Steady!" warned the Police officer.

Neither of the policemen mentioned the fact that Adam was wet, although they must have noticed.

It wasn't until after Adam had gone that I realised he had left his presents behind. I picked up one of the presents Adam had bought me and read the tag. *To Fay, with all my love, Adam xxx.* I wondered if he was sober when he wrote that. The writing seemed quite neat by Adam's standards. I wondered at what point he had started drinking again. Was it before or after he bought me the presents? I looked at the presents from me to Adam and was overwhelmed by a feeling of loss more profound than I had ever felt before. For I realised, possibly for the first time, that there truly was no hope for Adam, and no hope for us.

CHAPTER FIFTY-THREE

As Big Ben led the countdown to 2014 on the T.V., from outside I heard the sudden explosion of fireworks heralding the start of the New Year. I went over to the window and drew back the curtain. In the distance, a kaleidoscope of colours lit up the sky. I opened the window and breathed in the cool night air. Suddenly I felt a lump in my throat and tears welled in my eyes. For the first time that I could remember, the arrival of a New Year had real meaning. A mixture of sadness and hope as I finally said goodbye to my old life and my old self. I had been feeling as though my life were over and all that had made up me was spent, that I had nothing left to give. But now I was feeling something different, an inner strength perhaps. I wasn't going to let him destroy me. I would carry on. I would survive. I would no longer be a victim. Instead I would be victorious.

Suddenly I felt liberated. My future wasn't written yet and it could be anything I chose it to be. I was alone but I didn't need a man to define me. I was Fay, and there was no one like me in the whole wide world. I was unique, and I was special. This may have been the end of one story, but it was also the beginning of a new one.

As for Adam, I wished him the very best. However, his future was no longer mine and he had his own story to tell. I had been a part of it for a very long time, but now our paths would take us in different directions. I bore him no malice. I felt I could now look back and remember the good times when we were happy, but I had been trying to cling on to something that didn't exist anymore. I had to accept, we both needed to accept, that our story was now at an end. I realised then that I forgave him and I was finally ready to move on.

I turned around as I was suddenly aware of the familiar ring tone of my phone, almost drowned out by the sound of the fireworks. My phone was dancing along the desk where I had left it. I made my way across the room and picked it up.

"Happy New Year!" came a chorus of faceless yet familiar voices, as I lifted the phone to my ear.

I smiled. "Happy New Year to you too!"

And then a solitary voice. "How are you, Mom?"

"I'm fine, darling. I've Just been watching some fireworks from my window. Have you been out?"

"No," replied Ben. We invited some friends round for drinks earlier on. Then we just chilled in front of the tele. We let the girls stay up as long as they promised to be good."

"That's nice."

"The girls are desperate to speak to you, so I'll hand you over."

"Okay, Ben. Lovely to hear from you."

"Happy New Year, Granny Fay!" came a high-pitched voice.

"Is that Jessica?"

"No, it's Emily."

"Sorry, darling, you both sound the same on the phone."

"Mom and Dad let us stay up till midnight," said Emily, proudly.

"I know," I said. "Have you been good?"

"Yes," replied Emily, "we've been very good."

"I'm pleased to hear it."

"When are you coming back?"

"Soon," I replied.

"Wait! I'm talking to Granny Fay!"

"What is it, darling?"

"I've got to let Jessica talk to you now," said Emily, rather begrudgingly.

"Okay, darling, I'll see you soon! Be good!"

"Happy New Year!" came another familiar high-pitched voice.

"Is that Jessica?"

"Yeah!"

"I hear Mom and Dad let you stay up late?"

"Yeah, and we had champagne!"

"Really?"

"Well, just a sip really," said Jessica, rather disappointingly.

"Did you like it?"

"Nope, not really."

"Oh, well," I laughed. "I tell you what, when I come home, I'll take you and Emily out somewhere nice for a milk-shake. Maybe we could go to the cinema as well, if your Mom and Dad say it's okay."

"Yay!"

"You have to be good though," I warned.

"We will be."

"Okay, you better go now. Can you pass me over to Dad again?"

"Okay. Bye!"

"Bye, love!"

"Hi, Mom. What was Jessica so excited about?"

"I said I'd take her and Emily to the cinema and for a milk-shake when I get back, if that's okay?"

"Of course," replied Ben. "They always love spending time with their Granny Fay."

"I said they'd have to be good though," I added.

"I'm sure they will be."

"Yeah, they're good girls."

"Oh, Anita wants a quick word. So I'll say good-bye now, Mom."

"Okay, darling. Bye for now. And Happy New Year again."

“Hi, Fay! Happy New Year!”

“Happy New Year to you, Anita.”

“Are you having a nice break?”

“Yes, I am, I think. Thank you for ringing though. It’s lovely to speak to you all.”

“Well I really hope this year is going to be a better one for you. You’ve been through so much, you deserve some happiness now. I know Ben’s been so worried about you. And so have I, to be honest.”

“That’s sweet of you, but you and Ben no need to worry anymore. I’m going to be fine. In fact, I *am* fine.....*now*.”

“I’m so pleased to hear that, Fay.”

I crossed the room, then as I smiled knowingly at myself in the mirror on the wall, I said, “in fact, you know what, Anita? I think my new life is just beginning.”

Anita was silent for a moment, and although I couldn’t see her, I was certain she was smiling. “Have you been out anywhere tonight?” she asked.

“No,” I replied. “I had dinner in the restaurant earlier. Since then I have just been watching tele in my room.”

“That’s a shame,” said Anita. “Is there anything going on in the hotel?”

“I think the bar’s still open,” I said, glancing towards the door of my room, “and I can hear music coming from downstairs.”

“Why don’t you pop down there for a drink?” Anita suggested.

Now it was I who was silent for a moment. “Maybe I will,” I said.

After we said our good-byes, I quickly freshened up my make-up and took a deep breath before beginning to head downstairs. Just as I was locking the door however, something occurred to me. I returned to my room and with some difficulty, slid my wedding ring from my finger and placed it on the cupboard beside my bed. This was the first time I had removed my wedding ring in years, but now, this very moment, seemed to finally be the right time to do so. I looked at myself in the mirror again, as if to check whether my appearance had changed. But all I saw was the reflection of me. Fay. Not Fay Reynolds. Not Fay Matthews (*Matthews* was my maiden name). Just Fay. Not a unique name I know, but this particular Fay *was* unique. *I* was unique, with a unique story to tell. And as I continued to gaze at my reflection in the mirror, as though seeing myself for the first time, a mixture of conflicting feelings rushed through my veins: fear; trepidation; anticipation; overwhelmingly excitement. Excitement because I think I realised, as I began to smile knowingly again at my reflection in the mirror, that although one story may have come to an end, the very first words of the opening chapter of another unique story were about to be written.........

EPILOGUE

"Fay....Fay!" Someone was calling my name. I opened my eyes and turned my head towards the open window, the bright sunshine already streaming through a gap in the curtains, which fluttered and danced merrily in the breeze. I rolled over onto my side to find him gazing at me with his big brown beautiful eyes.

"Good morning," I smiled, sleepily. "What time is it?"

"Just after ten, he replied, huskily.

"We should get up."

"Not yet," he said as he wrapped his long muscular arms around me, holding me close in his strong yet gentle embrace. I snuggled up closer to him and buried my face in the thick dark hair of his chest. I could lie like this forever.

"Would you like a cuppa?"

I lifted my head as he released his embrace. "Yes, please, Darling," I half-whispered. I rolled back onto my back and sat up in bed, tucking the duvet under my bare arms. My eyes followed the long line of his brown toned body, as I watched him walk slowly towards the bedroom door. The sight of him still made me tingle all over. I never believed another man would want me again, especially a man as beautiful as he. But then *he* made me feel beautiful. *He* made me feel young again.

Whilst he was making the tea, I decided to get up. I slid my legs out from underneath the duvet and placed my feet on the rug beside the bed, burying my toes in its thick soft comforting pile. After tying the cord of my dressing gown loosely around my waist, I padded barefoot to the bathroom. The first thing I did was check my reflection in the mirror. I looked reasonably human, the smudged traces of last night's mascara still under my eyes.

After I had finished in the bathroom, I joined him in the living room. I sat down at one end of the corner sofa, just as he placed two mugs of tea on the coffee table before me. He had switched on the TV. I stared ahead at the screen, barely taking in whatever programme was on, as I cradled the steaming hot cup of tea in my hands, trying my hardest to wake up.

"Have you any plans today?" He was now sitting next to me on the sofa.

"Yeah, I'm meeting Jayne for lunch. Didn't I tell you?"

"Oh yes, I think you did," he replied.

"That's not a problem is it?"

"No, not at all," he said. "I'll pop for a quick drink with Jake." When he said *a quick drink*, I knew that was precisely what he meant. Unlike Adam, when *a quick drink* would always lead to another, and then another....

Jayne arrived punctually at 12.30 in her new red Volkswagen Polo. She had offered to drive us to a country pub where she and Mike had enjoyed a very nice, yet inexpensive meal one lunchtime. "It'll be my treat," Jayne had offered.

When we arrived, our table wasn't quite ready so we waited at the bar with our drinks, perched rather awkwardly on two rather rickety wooden stools. "So, how are things going with Luke?" Jayne asked.

"Oh, great," I replied, breezily. "I've never been happier."

Jayne smiled. "You seem very happy."

"Oh, I am." I smiled back knowingly, as I took a slow deliberate sip of my drink.

I'd grown accustomed to the life I had been dealt; my hopes, desires and dreams submerged and drowned in a sea of cynicism. But I realised now that the part that was no doubt the essence of me, had just turned cold and lay dormant all this time. I once believed that all my love was spent, but now the love inside me for this man was more than my heart could hold. And no man before him had ever made me feel so loved, so desired, and so safe. Not even Adam.

"Do you ever see anything of Adam these days?" Jayne asked, as though she were reading my mind.

"No, I haven't seen him for ages, fortunately. By all accounts, he's not doing too good."

"No, apparently not," said Jayne, rather solemnly.

“You mentioned something you wanted to tell me?” I said, digressing from the subject somewhat.

“Yes....” began Jayne, with a sense of hesitation in her voice. “I wasn’t sure whether or not to tell you at first, but then I thought, if it was me, would I want to know? And I think I would.”

“Know what?”

“Well, do you remember I was telling you about this course my boss was planning to send me on?”

“Yes....”

“Well, you never guess who I met there? Who was also on the course.”

“Who?” I wasn’t prepared to make a guess out of the 7.6 billion people living in the world.

“Debbie.”

“Debbie?” I echoed, furrowing my brows into a frown.

“Adam’s ex.”

My eyes now widened in realisation. “Are you sure it was her?”

“Oh, definitely. I wasn’t sure at first, not until we got chatting. She seems very nice by the way.” I merely raised my eyebrows. “But what you may find a bit surprising, is the reason why she left Adam in the first place.”

“Adam told me she left him for another man.”

“That’s what he told you.”

I gazed at Jayne, questioningly.

“Apparently Debbie had this old friend, Jack,” Jayne began to explain. “They’d been friends for years, ever since they were kids. But there was never anything between them, if you know what I mean. They were just good friends, like siblings really. Well Adam didn’t like it. He started accusing Debbie of cheating with Jack. Then one night, Debbie came home from an evening out with her girl friends and Adam accused her of being with Jack, of sleeping with him. Adam was drunk. They got into an argument and it ended up with him....well.... beating her up basically....quite badly apparently. And that was why she left.”

At first I was speechless, and then I managed to find my voice. “Do you believe her?”

“To be honest, Fay, I did.”

I emitted a huge sigh.

"Did Adam ever hit you?" asked Jayne, tentatively.

Looking down at my hands, I nodded. "Once."

I wasn't looking directly at Jayne, but I could visualise the shock on her face. I had never disclosed this to anyone before, not even to Jayne. "Do you want to talk about it?" Jayne's tone was softer now, more reassuring. Nevertheless, I still found it hard to look her directly in the eyes.

I shook my head. "Not now."

Jayne was silent but I could still feel her eyes on me, so I decided that it was up to me to break the awkward silence. "My only regret I think is not leaving sooner." I said, looking directly at Jayne now who was staring at me quite intently. "But then again, if I had, I probably would never have met Luke."

"You don't think so?"

"I doubt it. My choices and the path that I took would have been different."

"I suppose that's true," nodded Jayne.

A pretty young girl dressed smartly in a black shift dress, her dark hair tied up neatly in a bun, appeared beside us. "Your table is ready, if you'd like to follow me."

We followed the pretty young girl outside into the garden at the back of the pub, down a short flight of stone steps to a lawn overlooking the lake. We sat down opposite one another at the wooden picnic table. As I studied the menu, my mouth began to water in anticipation. I had missed breakfast and now I was feeling rather hungry.

"It's really lovely here," I remarked, as I gazed absently out at the lake, squinting in the sparkling reflection of the sun as it bounced off the ripples in the water. A family of wild ducks meandered their way through the reeds close to the bank. My eyes then wandered around the garden until they fixed upon something I was surprised I hadn't noticed before. At the foot of the steps we had just descended, a beautiful yellow rose bush was growing proudly against the brick stone wall. I smiled to myself and was surprised to find tears pricking my eyes.

"Fay? Are you okay?"

I turned my head to find Jayne gazing back at me with an expression of concern.

"I'm fine," I smiled, tears still glinting in my eyes. I can't say for certain whether they were tears of joy or sadness, of relief or regret. Or maybe it was because something I had read the other day suddenly had real poignancy. It was a feature in a magazine about the meaning of flowers. I discovered that the yellow rose can symbolise contentment and everlasting joy. Did I once feel that Adam and I shared just that? When the two of us made three. Our beautiful little family. But then the yellow rose can also symbolise a waning of passion, a bloodless love. Is that what eventually happened to us, to Adam and I? He may have continued to profess his love for me, but I knew that any feelings I once had for Adam had turned cold and bitter with the passage of time. Finally, the yellow rose can symbolise freedom and the promise of a new beginning. And I think that is the meaning I like best, and precisely what it meant to me now.

"Are you sure you're okay?" There was still some concern reflected in Jayne's eyes.

"Don't worry," I assured her, still smiling. "I'm honestly fine. More than fine. Now shall we order? I'm starving."

10607703R00120

Printed in Great Britain
by Amazon